Need Chocolate. And I need it now.

Ten minutes later, Mum caught me with my hand in the cookie jar.

"I thought you were off those this week," she said as she filled the kettle with water.

"I'm on a new diet," I said as I pushed a chocolate chip cookie into my mouth. "The seafood diet."

"What? Fish?"

"No, I see food and I eat it."

Mum laughed. "Well, at least you haven't lost your sense of humor."

Suddenly, I felt my eyes fill with tears and the cookie felt dry in my mouth.

"What is it, love?" Mum asked.

"Nothing," I said. "Just . . . I hate myself."

Mum looked aghast. "But why?"

"Look at me," I ____ ____ ____ on a diet and yet ____ soooo pathetic. N____

# Mates, Dates, and Chocolate Cheats

## Cathy Hopkins

Simon Pulse

New York   London   Toronto   Sydney

SIMON PULSE
An imprint of Simon & Schuster
Children's Publishing Division
1230 Avenue of the Americas, New York, NY 10020

Copyright © 2005 by Cathy Hopkins
Originally published in Great Britain in 2005
by Piccadilly Press Ltd.
Published by arrangement with Piccadilly Press Ltd.
All rights reserved, including the right of reproduction
in whole or in part in any form.

SIMON PULSE and colophon are registered
trademarks of Simon & Schuster, Inc.

Designed by Debra Sfetsios
The text of this book was set in Bembo.

Manufactured in the United States of America
First Simon Pulse edition January 2006
2 4 6 8 10 9 7 5 3

Library of Congress Control Number 2005925407
ISBN-13: 978-0-689-87696-7
ISBN-10: 0-689-87696-3

*Thanks as always to Brenda Gardner, Jon Appleton, Melissa Patey, and the team at Piccadilly Press. To Rosemary Bromley. And to Steve Lovering for his constant support, listening ear, and magical ability to produce chocolate then make it disappear in seconds.*

# Mates, Dates, and Chocolate Cheats

# Chapter 1

# The
# Flabmeister

"Mum," I called down the stairs. "My black jeans have shrunk in the wash."

Mum appeared from the kitchen. "Are you sure? They've never done that before."

"Maybe you put them on too hot a wash," I said as I went back into my room. It was the sort of thing that Mum would do without our cleaner Mrs. Dawson around to do things properly. Mum might be Mrs. Not-a-hair-out-of-place in her appearance and likes the house to be immaculate but domestically, she's a disaster. She's been known to turn a whole load of white washing blue or pink by mistake and she did pile all my clothes into the machine in a hurry after I got back from our school trip yesterday, so that I'd have something to wear today. It's a good job we don't have pets in this house as they'd probably have been shoved in the wash by mistake as well.

I lay back on the bed to try once again to get the zipper up on my jeans. I held my breath and pulled. . . . And held my breath and pulled again . . . but no way. The zipper was not going to budge. They had definitely shrunk. Poo, I thought. And these are my favorites too. My best jeans for making me look slimmer.

Just as I was rummaging around in my wardrobe, trying to find something else to wear, Mum appeared at my door.

"No luck?" she asked when she saw the discarded jeans on the floor.

I shook my head. "Nope. Definitely shrunk."

Mum shifted awkwardly about on her feet for a few moments. "Um, you don't think that by any chance you might have put on a little weight while you were in Italy?" she asked.

"No way," I said. "With all that walking around Florence, I think I must have *lost* weight. I mean, it wasn't as though we exactly pigged out." Except for the ice cream and pizza and pasta and . . . oh dear, better go and weigh myself, I thought as I headed for the bathroom.

I crossed my fingers and got on the scales.

"No way," I gasped when I saw the reading. "No *way*. They *have* to be wrong."

Mum was hovering outside the bathroom. "Well?" she asked.

"Scales are wrong," I said as I passed her on my way out. "Quite clearly nothing in this house is working properly."

Mum smiled. "Don't worry about it. You look fine."

She doesn't understand. How could she when she looks like a rake and can eat as much as she likes without putting on an ounce?

"Do not," I said. "This is a *major* disaster."

Back in my room, I took a long look at myself in the mirror. Back, front, sideways. Yuck. It's too horrible. Flab, flab, flabby. People used to say that I looked like Alanis Morissette with my dark hair and tall, slim shape, but not any longer, I thought as I pulled in my tummy as far as it would go. The only celebrity I resemble now is Miss Piggy. Oh rat rot. I have definitely put on weight and I can't blame the mirror.

I did a quick addition in my head. Okay, so I put on five pounds over Christmas and New Year. But everyone puts on a few pounds over that time and it wasn't exactly my fault—so many people bought me boxes of chocolate. It would have been impolite not to eat them. And with all the other stuff around at that time of year: pudding, mince pies, roast potatoes, turkey, stuffing . . . how can anyone not gain a little weight? But another three pounds at half-term on the school trip? How did *that* happen? Five and three. That's eight pounds. Five pounds I could just about get away with but eight? Definitely not. In Italy, we only had a tiny mirror in the hotel bathroom so I hadn't noticed the full extent of the damage but now I'm home, I can see properly. And it's serious. That's it. I'm never going out again. No way can I be seen in public looking like this. So no going out. Not until I've dropped it. No. I shall hide under the bed and starve until I'm fit to be seen again.

"Izzie," Mum called. "Get a move on. I'm not

going to wait all day for you and we're late as it is."

Knickers, I thought as I pulled on a pair of my old baggy jeans. Something has to change round here. And fast.

When I got to school, I waited at the gates for my mates, Nesta, TJ, and Lucy. We'd all been on the school trip and I was dying to know what had happened after we'd got home last night. It had been amazing at the airport. We'd just come through the arrivals lounge when TJ spotted a boy with the most enormous bunch of roses at the end of the line of people awaiting passengers. It was Tony, Lucy's ex (and Nesta's brother). They'd had a big fall-out just before we'd left for Florence and the relationship was off but then, there he was with the flowers at the airport and he whizzed her away. It was so romantic.

I'd called Nesta for an update as soon as I got home last night and all she knew was that Tony was over at Lucy's. And we'd all called Lucy but her mobile was switched off and when we tried the landline, her brother, Lal, said she was busy and wasn't to be disturbed. Remind me to kill him when I see him, the rat, I thought. I bet he had his ear glued to her door all evening. He's a nosy parker and is always butting into our business especially anything to do with our love lives. Probably because he doesn't have one of his own. Anyway, by bedtime, the breaking news on the Tony and Lucy situation was they were still in "conference." Probably a snog conference if you asked me. But talk about suspense. It was killing me.

After a few moments, I saw Nesta's dad's BMW draw up by the bus stop. I had to smile when I saw her get out of the back. She was dressed in black with a black shawl tossed over her shoulders, her hair pulled back into a ponytail, and even though it was a dismal February day, she was still wearing the big Gucci sunglasses that she'd borrowed from her mum for the trip. With her exotic looks (half-Italian, half-Jamaican) she is stunning most of the time but today she looked every inch an Italian *Vogue* model. Typical Nesta. She likes to make an entrance, even if it's only into school assembly.

"Never forget, dahling," she drawled in a fake Italian accent as she came to join me and took off the glasses, "that wherever we are, we must never forget our sense of style."

"Yeah, right," I said as I saw her glance over my baggy outfit.

"I thought we'd decided to go mega sophisticated after Italy," she said. "You decided to go back to the grunge look?"

"Mum put my jeans in the wash and they shrunk and all my other stuff wasn't dry . . ."

"Rotten to be back, isn't it?" she interrupted as she leaned against the gate post and put her glasses back on.

"Tell me about it," I said as I spotted TJ getting off the bus and waving at us.

"Hey," she said as she came over. "Doesn't this seem unreal? Like, straight back to the old routine. Already Italy seems like a dream."

At least TJ was dressed normally. A week in the one of the most fashionable places in Europe and she still favored jeans and a sweatshirt. But she looked so slim in them. Pig poo, I thought, I wonder if anyone has noticed that I have turned into the flabmeister.

Nesta wrapped her shawl tighter around herself.

"I know," she said. "They should have given us another week off to adjust to being back in England. It feels so much colder here."

"So?" I asked. "What's the gossip on Lucy and Tony? Anyone seen her yet?"

Nesta rolled her eyes. "All I know is that Tony was over at her house all yesterday evening. He got home late and locked himself in his room and this morning, he'd already gone by the time I got up. You know what he's like, not exactly Mr. Communication when it comes to spilling the beans on his love life."

"All evening?" I asked. "Sounds like it's back on."

"Maybe," said TJ. "So I guess we'd better get ready for the roller coaster ride again."

Tony and Lucy have been on off, on off for well over a year. The trouble usually starts when Tony starts pushing Lucy further than she wants to go in the bedroom department. That's why they split up last time because she said no way José and he said he couldn't take it. Part of the problem is that he's eighteen and she's not even fifteen yet and she felt she wasn't ready to sleep with him. They do make a strange-looking couple really because Tony's tall and dark and Lucy is tiny (or petite as she likes to say) and looks like a blonde pixie. Just before we left for Florence, he decided that it wasn't going to work but he obviously changed his mind while we were away.

As the bell for assembly rang, there was still no sign of Lucy and although we lingered as long as we could, in the end we had to go in or else risk a detention.

In double English that morning, Lucy still hadn't shown so I reconciled myself with having to wait until break to phone her. Mr. Johnson, our teacher (also fresh back from Florence) went for the easy option. Easy for him, anyway. He asked us to write an essay on "What I Did on my Holidays." How predictable is that after a break? I thought. Then he fell asleep.

"Frescoed out in Florence," I wrote as my title.

After twenty minutes, I had only written four lines.

Walked a lot.

Saw a load of churches and frescos.

Ate a lot. (Oh dear, but v. enjoyable at the time.

Who was it said a moment on the lips, a lifetime on the hips? I'd like to meet them so I could kill them.)

Snogged my face off. (I met this fab boy called Jay on the plane going out. He was on a school trip too and his party was staying at the same hotel as us. At first I thought it was fate bringing us together then we found out that all the schools in North London always book into the same hotel because they get a cheap package deal. Flight and room for ze 'orrible Engleesh teenagers sort of thing. Anyway, his school isn't too far from ours so . . . watch this space. I really hope to see him again.)

I rubbed out the last bit as I didn't reckon Mr. Johnson would want to read about my snog fests and tried to put my mind to my essay. It's hard when you've had a week off. Like the battery in my brain had gone flat. I looked over at Nesta and TJ to see what they were up to. TJ was scribbling madly. Pff. She would be. She loved Florence and she loves history and English and all that sort of thing. She's a brainbox really. Her e-mail address is babewithbrains as she's quite a babe too, even though she doesn't think so but boys always notice her. She has lovely thick long, dark hair and a full, wide mouth that could be used to advertize collegen injections. Only hers is *au naturel*.

Nesta looked as bored as I was. She made her eyes go cross, pulled a face and flicked her rubber at me with her ruler.

"Ouch," I cried as it hit me on the side of the head and unfortunately Mr. Johnson woke up.

"Wh . . . where . . . what . . . ?" he stuttered as he came out of his reverie.

He clearly hadn't quite landed either.

As soon as the bell went for break, we were out, down the corridor and I called Lucy double quick.

"Hey, skiver," I said when I got through. "What's happening?"

"Mum thought I still looked peaky after my food poisoning in Florence so told me to take the day off."

"Pff," I said. "Lucky you. But I meant what's *happening* happening?"

"Oh . . . er . . . she said I have to drink lots of fluids . . ."

"I mean with *Tony*?"

"And rest . . ."

"Oh. Ah . . . Is someone there? You can't talk?"

"No. I mean yes. My mum's here playing Florence Nightingale. Hey, I wonder if she ever went to Florence. Florence Nightingale I mean. Then she'd have been Florence in Florence."

"Shut up, Lucy. You are clearly delirious. Shall we come over after school?"

"Yeeesssss."

After school, I dropped off my holiday film at the chemist's and we all headed straight over to Lucy's.

She was sitting up in bed, surrounded by glossy mags and was painting her nails turquoise blue. She looked absolutely fine. Better than fine. Rested and relaxed and she'd clearly had time to do her hair and now her nails. Huh. Some people.

"Oh thank God you're here," she said. "I've been so bored."

"Well, you look all right to me," said Nesta as she sat on the end of her bed. "So don't expect any sympathy. You get a day off and the rest of us have had to suffer the tortures of double English and double maths, all on the same day. Life just isn't fair sometimes."

I laughed. Nesta would make a rotten nurse.

"How are you?" asked TJ who would make a good nurse as she's always aware of others and what they're going through.

"Okay, thanks," said Lucy. "But I did feel a bit queasy this morning. Honestly."

"Yeah right," said Nesta. "So? Spill. What's going on with you and my ratfink brother?"

"Close the door," said Lucy.

TJ quickly did as she asked and we all looked at Lucy in anticipation.

"So?" repeated Nesta.

"Nothing," said Lucy.

"Nothing?" asked Nesta. "What's that supposed to mean?"

"I told him I wasn't going back with him. I mean, one bunch of flowers and I'm supposed to fall at his feet. Give me a break."

"Wow," said TJ. "I would have. I thought it was so romantic."

"Yeah, but it doesn't really change things," said Lucy.

"So why was he there?" asked TJ. *"Avec les fleurs?"*

"He said he'd done a lot of thinking while I was

away and he'd realized that he'd rather be with me and not have sex than be with someone he doesn't really care about and do it."

"Good for him," I said. "He really, really does like you, doesn't he?"

"And I like him," said Lucy. "That will never change. But I'm not going back to where we were before. I mean, get real. How long before he gets restless and starts with the wandering hands again? A month? A week?"

"A day, knowing my brother," said Nesta. "No, an hour."

"Exactly," said Lucy.

"So what now?" asked TJ.

"We move on," said Lucy. "Florence really helped me do that. I told him that I'm not going back."

"How did he take it?" I asked.

Lucy grinned. "Said he's not going to give up."

Nesta sighed and flopped back on the bed. "Oh, here we go again."

"No, really," said Lucy. "I can be quite stubborn when I want to be. I really mean it. And anyway, he'll be going to university in September so we'd probably break up then anyway."

"But that's ages away," I said. "Almost seven months."

"So?" said Lucy. "If we got back together, can you imagine? I'd spend seven months dreading September so I'm moving on now."

Nesta sat up again. "Okay. Good. You move on. We all move on. A new chapter in all our books. So let's review the situation." She looked over at me. "Miss Foster, take a note."

I poised myself with an imaginary pad and pen in secretary mode, ready for her plan. Nesta's big on plans and big on getting everyone to join in with them.

"Okay," said Nesta. "Lucy. Free. Find new boy."

"Er, not necessarily," said Lucy.

"Miss Foster, scratch that memo," said Nesta. "Lucy. Free. No boy."

"Not necessarily that, either. I want to stay open."

Nesta sighed. "Okay. Lucy. Confused as always. Moving on. TJ. You going to see that Liam guy you met on holiday again?"

TJ shrugged. "Nah. Don't think so. Maybe as a mate but nothing else. No chemistry."

"Okay. TJ. Free. You want a new boy?"

TJ shrugged again. "Maybe, maybe not."

Nesta sighed heavily. "God, get a life, you guys. Show me some enthusiasm here. Okay. Me. No boy. Love of my life left in *Italia* and he can't write English so no chance of any love letters. Not good but hey, as Lucy said, life must go on and that's precisely why I brought this issue of boys up. My philosophy is that the best way to get over one is to find a distraction. Preferably another boy."

I laughed. Didn't take her long to recover, I thought. On the plane coming back, it was Marco this and Marco that, but then she had only pulled him on the last night so it wasn't exactly like they'd had a whole week to fall truly in love. Lucy on the other hand, had spent almost the whole week with someone—a lovely American boy called Teddy who she'd hooked up with, but then he lives on the other side of the world, so not much chance of that coming to anything while they're both at school.

"Hey, did you tell Tony about Teddy?" I asked.

"No way," she replied. "At least, not the whole truth. I said we met a load of boys while we were there and spent some time hanging out with them and having a laugh. He didn't seem to want details, which was a relief and as Teddy lives in the States, it's not likely to come up."

"Yes," said Nesta. "We need boys who live locally."

"So what about William, Nesta?" I asked. "Not like you to let someone as cute as him slip away."

Nesta grimaced. "Luke's mate? Yes. I did consider him for a nanosecond but crossed him off the list. Friend of Luke's. Don't want to go anywhere near there again."

TJ looked at the floor. I think she still felt uncomfortable about the "Luke" situation. Before Christmas, he'd been going out with Nesta and then he made a play for TJ and I think she genuinely did fall in love with him and thought he was her soulmate. It all got v. complicated and almost split us up as mates, because I sided with TJ and Lucy sided with Nesta. In the end we all decided that it wasn't worth losing our friendship over a boy who couldn't be trusted. I think it left TJ feeling a bit bruised though and she doesn't like to talk about him much. Shame about William. We only met him after it was all over and he seemed really nice and clearly fancied Nesta. But I understood her reluctance to get involved with him, being Luke's friend and all.

"Izzie? What about you?" asked Nesta. "You going to see Jay?"

"Hope so," I said. I decided that now was the time to ask the question that I'd been wanting to ask all day. "Hey, listen guys. I need you to tell me something and I want you to be really, *really* honest. . . ."

"Sounds serious," said Nesta.

"It is. I want you to tell me, do you think I've put on weight?"

Nesta, Lucy and TJ looked at each other.

"No," said TJ after a moment too long. "Not really. Well, we all did a little. So no more than the rest of us."

"Is that a yes or a no?"

"You look great, as always," said Lucy, ever my ally. "Don't even think about it."

"Well, I have to. My jeans don't fit."

"Okay . . ." said Nesta. "Seeing as no one around here is telling the truth, yes you have put on a little weight. I noticed in Italy, actually, and didn't want to say anything but . . ."

"Nesta," interrupted Lucy. "You are always putting your foot in your mouth. In fact you only ever open your mouth to change feet."

"Hey, that's not fair," said Nesta. "You didn't even let me finish. Yes, Izzie, you have put on a little weight but no big deal. You can carry it. You're the tallest of us all, so no biggie."

"Hmph. I'd say it is a biggie. And I'm the biggie, to be precise. Tell me honestly, do I look fat?"

"No way," TJ and Lucy chorused.

"Am I as big as Angela Roberts in Year Eleven?" I stood up and stuck my stomach out for them. "See, I look pregnant."

"No way," said TJ. "That's a huge exaggeration."

"Okay, so is it my bum or my tum or my legs that look biggest?"

TJ and Nesta exchanged a look and the next thing I knew, they had pulled a pillow out from behind Lucy, wrestled me to the floor and shoved the pillow over my face.

"For heaven's sake, shut up about being fat," said Nesta. "Not fat, not fat, not fat. You are curvy."

Curvy? I thought as I tried to fight them off. Curvy? That's just a polite way of saying fat. Curvy. Oh dog doo.

Suddenly I wished I hadn't asked.

I got home later to the alluring smell of garlic and onions. Mum had been doing pasta in a tuna and tomato sauce with parmesan cheese. Calorific and a half. No way could I eat that even though I was hungry. I'd hardly eaten all day. As Nesta and TJ had tucked into their sandwiches at lunch-time, I had binned mine and just eaten my apple. Then, later at Lucy's when her mum brought us up tea and cookies, I hadn't had one.

I quickly checked that Mum and Angus (my stepdad) were busy watching TV then went back to the kitchen. This is how it has to be, I thought, as I binned my supper and hid it under some newspaper so that Mum wouldn't notice. Then I made myself two ryvitas with a scraping of marmite. I have to accept that I have to suffer to be beautiful. When I went to bed a couple of hours later, my stomach was rumbling and all I could think of was food. The song from the musical *Oliver!* began to sing in my brain, *"Food glorious food . . . hot bangers and mustard . . . While we're in the mood, baked apple and custard . . ."* Or something like that. Plates of steaming pasta, baked potatoes with lashings of butter, slices of toast and peanut butter, chocolate cake and blueberry muffins began to play across the screen of my mind. I am *starving*, I thought as my body seemed to rise of its own accord from the bed like a sleepwalker and make its way down the stairs and into the kitchen where it began to raid the fridge. I'll start properly tomorrow, I thought as I made myself a hot chocolate, then ate my way through a huge chunk of wholemeal bread with peanut butter and damson jam, two cookies, and a piece of marzipan-covered cake.

Phew, that feels better, I thought as I went back to bed full of good resolutions for the morning.

> Eat, drink, and be merry, for tomorrow,
> we may diet.

# Teen
# Talk

"Don't you keep your mobile on?" asked Nesta when I got to the school gates the next day. "I've been trying to ring you all morning."

Lucy and TJ were already there hanging out with her and trying to delay the moment of actually having to go in for as long as possible. Even though it was cold and drizzly, we all preferred to be outside rather than in.

"I only spoke to you last night," I said as I rubbed my arms to try and keep warm. "What could possibly have happened since then that can't wait?"

"Opportunity of a lifetime," she said with a grand sweep of her hands. "My dad told me at breakfast this morning. He was having a drink with one of his producer friends last night and he told him about a new telly program he's launching and he wants teens to be in it. Us. We can go for it."

"Er, slow down a moment, Nesta," said TJ. "One slight problem. Like we have to come to school."

"And we're not actresses," said Lucy.

"Not a problem. It's going to happen on a Saturday. It's going to be called *Teen Talk*, a discussion show sort of thing, and they want teens in the audience to participate and a few for a panel to give their views . . ."

"Views on what?" asked Lucy.

Nesta shrugged. "Dunno. Life. Dunno. Who cares? They want opinions, we have them, and if we haven't got them, we'll get them. Anyway, he asked Dad if we'd be interested in going to the preliminary meeting on Thursday. They're seeing a whole bunch of people and are going to pick about thirty and then they'll film a pilot episode in a couple of Saturdays' time. You up for it?"

"You bet," said Lucy.

"Not me and anyway, I can't do Saturdays," said TJ. "I have the magazine to do at the weekends and I'm a bit behind now after the Italy trip."

TJ edits the school magazine, *For Real*, with Emma Ford from Year Eleven. They do a brilliant job but it's time consuming for TJ and often she can't hang out with the rest of us on a Saturday because of it.

"Oh, can't you get out of it?" asked Nesta. "It will be so top. All of us together. A real laugh. Get Emma to do the magazine for a few weeks."

TJ shook her head. "I can't leave her with it. She'd kill me. Anyway, you know being on TV isn't my kind of thing. I don't mind writing opinions down but I turn into Noola the Alien Girl if I have to say much in public."

We all laughed. We knew Noola, TJ's alter ego, well. TJ, who is easily the brainiest of us all, comes out with this strange language (she calls it Outerspaceagongalese) if she's put on the spot and particularly when she meets a cute boy. It was hysterical the first time we witnessed it. It was when she met Tony and started mumbling alien speak. She could only say words like "uh" or "nihwee" or "ug."

"What about you, Izzie? You in?" asked Nesta.

"Yeah, maybe." I nodded, but in my head I'd

gone into a panic. I'd read somewhere that the television camera adds ten pounds to your weight. Ten plus the five at Christmas plus the three from the Italian trip. That's eighteen pounds. Oh god. I'd look enormous. But on the other hand, I'd really love to do it. Oh hell. Maybe I'll be able to drop the weight in time for the pilot. "What's the first meeting for exactly?" I asked.

"It's for the producers to check that we're not mad and likely to do something weird like strip naked and run in front of the cameras waving our knickers in the air . . ."

"As if," I said. "We'd wear them on our heads like normal people."

Lucy and TJ laughed, but Nesta ignored what I'd said and continued.

"Then if we get selected, there's the first run-through on Saturday. If the pilot is a goer, they'll go into production in the autumn. Oh come on, guys. We have to do it. It could be our first break. You never know who might be watching the show. We could be discovered and on our way to the bright lights of Hollywood."

"Yeah, right," I said. "And pigs might fly."

"No, we'll come. Won't we, Iz?" asked Lucy.

"Yeah. Sure," I said. They usually pick a whole variety of people for audiences to represent all backgrounds and types. ·

I could be the token fat person.


After school, I took a detour to the local newsagent's on the way home and spent a good chunk of my pocket money on magazines. I knew exactly what I was looking for. Ones that said anything like "Lose ten pounds in ten easy steps" with a picture of a skinny girl holding up her old ginormous pair of trousers to show how she'd shrunk ten sizes—that kind of thing. Luckily there were loads.

I raced home, up to my bedroom, and began to read.

The Atkins diet, sounds good. Good results. No carbs, only protein. Hmm. Could be difficult as I'm vegetarian. Maybe I could eat meat just for a few weeks. No. Can't. Even though I'm desperate, I still couldn't eat one of those sweet baby lambs' legs or chew my way through a cow's buttock. *Bleurghh*. Maybe I could eat just fish. That's protein. And supposed to be good for the brain. Fish for supper every night? Ohmicod. Maybe not. What else is there?

The next magazine raved on about the Hay diet. I hoped that wasn't just eating hay but no, it was all about not mixing your carbohydrates and your proteins at the same meal. That sounded more do-able and seemed like a healthy option. Tick. I'll do that. What else?

"Eat Right for Your Blood Type," said the next mag. Some celebrities swear by it.

"Mum," I called down the stairs. "What blood type am I?"

"I have no idea," she called back. "Red, like the rest of us. Why? Are you thinking of becoming a vampire?"

Oh, very funny. Mum's discovered she has a sense of humor. Not, I thought as I went back to my magazine and read more about that diet. Nope, sounds too complicated. You have to have a blood test to find out what kind of blood you are and I hate needles.

Bananas and milk one day, eggs and grapefruit the next. Some of the models use it when they need a quick fix. Tick. Might try that one.

The cabbage diet. Yuck. I hate cabbage. But tick. Might try that one.

No carbs after midday. Tick. Easy. I'll do that as well.

Drink at least six glasses of water a day to help eliminate toxins and keep your digestive system working well. Tick. Do that.

And low fat everything. Tick. Do that.

Hmm. But if I'm on the Atkins diet, that says I can have cheese and cream and butter. That's high fat.

Now I'm getting confused.

"Izzie," Mum called from the kitchen. "Supper's on the table."

This is going to be interesting, I thought as I put my magazines aside and went down.

She'd made cheesy baked potatoes and salad. Healthy enough but . . .

"Sorry, Mum, but I can't eat that," I said as I sat at the table.

"Why not?" asked Mum as she served out pork chops for her and Angus.

"I'm not eating carbs after midday anymore," I explained. "And I'm on the Hay diet so I can't mix my carbohydrates and my proteins."

Mum sighed. "And why is that?"

I pinched a good wedge of flab on my hips and stuck my stomach out for her. "Isn't it obvious? I'm enormous. I have to go on a diet. And the Hay diet says . . ."

Angus laughed. "But there's nothing of you. You don't need to diet."

He is clearly blind.

"I'll eat the salad," I said while I tried to decide whether to have the cheese or the potato. Maybe the potato because cheese is high fat but if I'm on the Atkins, cheese would be all right. But then, if I had the potato, it's carbohydrate and I'd decided not to have carbs after midday. Oh hell, this isn't going to be easy. Maybe I'll just stick with the salad.

"Have you put dressing on the salad? Because I'm also only having low fat stuff from now on."

Mum rolled her eyes and Angus grimaced and began to eat his meal. I think he knew what was coming, as I did. A lecture.

"Low fat products are often high in sugar and have more calories. Anyway, you do *not* need to go on a diet, Isobel," Mum began. (I always know that she's serious when she calls me Isobel.) "You might have a bit of puppy fat on you but you're a growing girl and it will soon—"

"Growing in *all* directions, Mum. I have to do something about it. And I'm fifteen. Way past the puppy fat stage."

"Izzie, I have bent over backwards to get you food that you *will* eat. First it was no meat. And then it was we have to eat more healthy food. I've done that. And now you want to do the Hay diet or whatever. No. I'm not having it. Nor any other mad fad diets. You will eat sensibly and that's the end of it. A baked potato is very healthy and not going to put weight on you. Have it without the butter if you must but you *will* eat something."

There are times when there's no point in arguing with Mum. And this was one of them. I have learned (from Nesta) that if I need to get her to agree to something, the best time to get her is when she's watching one of her favorite TV programs and doesn't want to be disturbed. She'll agree to anything then if only to get me to shut up.

"Okay," I said as I cut a tiny piece of my potato

up and put it in my mouth. "You know best. Er . . . what's on TV tonight?"

Mum gave Angus a "what's going on?" look but he just shrugged. He tries to stay out of our arguments.

"Why?" she asked.

"Nothing. Oh . . . talking of telly. One of Nesta's dad's mates is launching a new TV show and they want teens for the audience. He asked if we'd like to be part of it, so can I go? They're selecting on Thursday and they'll do a run through on Saturday. It's a sort of discussion show thing. Very intellectual. And . . . be, er . . . great work experience."

Mum put her knife and fork down. "No. I don't think so."

"Why not?"

"You've just been to Italy for a week. You're behind on your homework and need to catch up."

I was about to object but could see that her back had stiffened and she was sitting up very straight as if primed for a fight. She was definitely in "no" mood. Take a deep breath, I told myself. Pick your time. I took another mouthful of my potato. "Okay," I said. "I guess I do need to catch up on schoolwork."

She gave me a suspicious look but I smiled back sweetly. I'll get her later when she's ensconced in the telly, I thought. Oh ja. Ve have vays of making you give in.

> The skipping diet: Skipping breakfast, skipping lunch, skipping supper.

# Chapter 3

# The Tummy Song

Wednesday weigh-in. Arrghhhhhh. I'd put on half a pound since Monday! How could that have happened?

Drastic measures are called for, I thought, as I had half a grapefruit and a boiled egg for breakfast, followed by two large glasses of water. Mum tried to get me to have cereal as well, so I poured myself a bowl, then poured it back into the packet when she was in the hall spraying posh hairspray all over her hair (which is cut into such a perfect bob that it doesn't need spray to keep it in place). I think

Angus saw me as he was making himself some toast but he didn't say anything.

School was unbelievably embarrassing as halfway through PHSE, my stomach decided to sing the tummy song. Gurgle, wurgle, woggle, schlosh. And it wasn't just once. It went on and *on*. I went bright purple and tried breathing in and even holding my breath but schlosh, schlosh it went. A few girls started giggling and then a few more and even Miss Watkins began laughing in the end. And it takes a lot to get her to laugh.

"Someone's tummy is hungry," she said finally. "Did you miss breakfast, Izzie?"

"No, Miss," I said as the whole class stared at me. "Must have a bug." A whole family of them in fact, I thought as my tummy gurgle-wurgled again.

Later, when we were changing for gym, I felt even worse. All around me, my classmates were gaily stripping off without a care in the world while I tried to change with my back turned to them all so that no one would notice that I had turned into Mrs. Blobby. They were all so *skinny*. At five foot eight, I must be the tallest in our class now plus my boobs have taken on a life of their own and are expanding at twice the rate of the universe. Soon I won't be able to see my feet! And my bum. Oh, it's *too* sad. I couldn't believe it, even Candice Carter's tummy was as flat as a pancake and she's pregnant. It was the big scandal just before we left for Italy and I did feel sorry for her. She was out of her mind with worry about what her parents were going to say and what she was going to do. She'd been sleeping with her steady boyfriend for a while and she told us that they'd always used condoms but one time, the condom must have burst or leaked or whatever they do when it all goes wrong.

When she'd gone into the showers, I nudged Lucy.

"Amazing, isn't it, I look three months pregnant and Candice doesn't look as if she's having a baby at all."

"She's not anymore," whispered Lucy. "Apparently she lost it. Miscarriage."

"God. How awful. Or is it?"

Lucy did a quick check to see that she wasn't coming back in. "I think it's a relief actually. You know she wasn't ready to be a single mum. And she wants to go to college, remember?"

I did remember. We'd found her in the cloak-rooms one day sobbing her heart out as she considered her options. It was a real wake-up call for everyone as although most of our year haven't slept with boys yet, we've all certainly been thinking about it. Lucy told me in Italy that seeing Candice so distraught was what made her sure that she wasn't ready to sleep with Tony. She didn't want to risk it and maybe end up going through what had happened to Candice.

At lunch, while I had my grapefruit (hmm, yummy, not), the others had sandwiches, crisps, and *chocolate. Soooo* unfair. My mouth was watering, but I stuck to my resolve and didn't have any, even though they all told me I was mad to be on a diet and kept waving bits of chocolate in front of my nose. It's all right for them. All of them are thin with no wobbly bits at all. To distract myself from watching them wolf down their food, I pulled out my photos from the Italian trip which I'd picked up on the way to school.

We'd already looked at them first thing, then again at break but another look wouldn't hurt as the pics brought Italy (and Jay) back into sharp focus. Although the trip was over, I couldn't help but think that one part of it had come back on the plane with me. And I don't mean my memories (cue romantic violins), no, I mean the five foot ten gorgeous Indian boy by the name of Jay. He looked so good in the photos and seeing them made me want to meet up with him again as soon as possible. Unlike Florence, he wasn't far away, probably at his school in North London, maybe looking at his own photos at the same time as TJ, Nesta, Lucy, and I looked at mine. Probably thinking, who's that great fairy elephant standing next to me in my pictures? I hoped not, as I think he did like me.

"They say that the camera doesn't lie but I wish sometimes it would fib a little," I said as I looked at one particularly unflattering shot of me bending over to tie my trainers outside the Duomo. I made a mental note to rip it up or put it on the fridge as a reminder of why I had to keep to my diet.

"What do you mean?" asked Lucy.

"Duh. I look enormous."

"No you don't," said TJ. "The camera just got you at a bad angle, that's all. You looked great in Italy and the boys there really liked your green eyes. Remember in the Piazza della Signoria where they kept saying *bella ochi*, beautiful eyes."

"Yeah, because that's the only part of me that's okay at the moment. My eyes, my ear lobes and maybe my little toes. The rest of me is . . ."

"Oh for God's sake, Izzie," Lucy interrupted. "For the last time, you are *not* fat."

I noticed Nesta wasn't making any comment as she flipped through the photos. Probably couldn't trust herself not to say something insulting.

"Have you heard from Jay?" she asked finally as she got to the end of the pile.

I shook my head. It would be so cool to see him again and pick up where we left off. The end of the holiday had come round so fast and then there was the flight home and being met at the airport. I hadn't thought about swapping numbers or arranging to see him again over here until it was too late. And now I wished that I had. Being with him had made the Italian trip extra special and we had got on really well. We'd talked about everything: our families, past relationships, what music we liked, fave foods, TV programs, what we wanted to do after we'd left school, why God didn't sort out some of the mess us humans have made down here. We'd got really close.

"Well, it's only Wednesday," said Lucy. "Give the boy a break. You know what they're like. When a mate says she'll phone, she means probably in an hour. When a boy says he'll phone, he means sometime, maybe in a week and that's if I remember."

"Have you heard from Teddy?" I asked.

She nodded. "Yeah, he's e-mailed a couple of times."

"See," said Nesta. "If a boy says he'll phone, if he likes you, you don't have to wait too long. I've already heard from a few boys from the trip."

My heart sank. I knew she was right. If a boy likes you, he phones. Okay, maybe not as fast as a girl would phone, but he phones.

"Actually . . . Jay didn't take my number," I said. "We both forgot."

"I could get it for you," said Nesta. "Eddie phoned. Remember him? The one with red hair and the high forehead? He was a mate of Jay's."

"And Liam called me," said TJ. "I could get it from him as well."

"*Noooo.* Don't," I said. If I could get Jay's number

39

this easily, I thought, he could have got mine. So why hadn't he? I cast my mind back to the last time I'd seen him. It was at the airport and we were waiting for our luggage. It had all been such a rush with trolleys and people bashing into one another as they hauled their cases about. I remember he thanked me for a fab time in Florence and said I'd made the trip really special for him. And then Liam thought it would be funny to ride round on the carousel along with the cases and everyone started laughing when one of the security men dived on after him. Jay and Eddie darted forward to try and pull Liam off so that he didn't get into trouble and after that, everything went into a blur, like a DVD on fast forward. I spotted my case and moved in to collect it, there was a big commotion with the security guard, the boys, and one of their teachers and when I looked for Jay again, he and his mates were being escorted by their angry looking teacher towards the arrival gate. Not exactly the best time to get someone's number.

"Why not let Nesta get it for you?" asked Lucy. "You clearly both liked each other a lot and he might be waiting to hear from you."

I shook my head. "I don't want to seem too

keen. He could get my number if he wanted."

"Quite right," said Nesta. "Treat 'em mean to keep 'em keen. That's my motto."

Lucy laughed. "Yeah right, it's your motto until *you're* keen and then you're as bad as the rest of us."

Nesta chose to ignore her comment. "But listen, Izzie," she said, "a bunch of the boys from the trip are meeting up in Crouch End after school. Eddie asked if I wanted to go along. Let's all go for half an hour or so. And Chris and Liam will be there . . ."

Lucy grimaced. "No thanks. You can count me out of this one," she said when Nesta mentioned Chris's name. He'd tried to pull her on the trip and she didn't fancy him. It all culminated in him pushing an envelope with a condom in it with a note saying *Tonight's your lucky night* under the door for her one night. She'd filled the condom with water to make a water bomb and smashed it over his head in reply. I could understand her reluctance to meet up with him again.

"And anyway," she continued, "I said I'd meet Tony."

"I thought that it was over between you," I said. "Remember? You're moving on?"

"We can still be friends," said Lucy sheepishly.

Nesta rolled her eyes. "Yeah, right," she said.

"I know you don't believe me but it is just friends. Like—he wanted to come to the *Teen Talk* thing with us tomorrow and I told him no, I want to do some things on my own. So see, I am being independent."

"So why are you seeing him tonight?" I asked.

"He wants to talk over his university options with me," said Lucy. "He's had a couple of offers but isn't sure where he wants to go. He was talking about staying here and going to one in London so that we could still be together."

"See," said Nesta. "I knew it. He's wheedling his way back in."

"He might have had offers," I said. "But he still has to get the results they ask for."

"He'll get his results," said Lucy. "He's really clever."

"Yeah, he is," said Nesta. "Just look how clever he is at getting you back. Oh, Lucy, please come and help me decide which university I should go to. I think I ought to go to one near you. It's just an excuse to get you over to our flat and into his bedroom."

"I can look after myself," said Lucy. "And I'm

not going to let what's happening with us or not happening with us determine which university he goes to. He must go to the one that's best for him and I'm going to tell him that."

"Huh. So you say, but don't blame me if it ends in tears," said Nesta, and then she turned to me. "But you should come out with TJ and me, Iz. Jay hangs out with those boys so he might be there as well. You can check out the situation without him feeling like you're closing in on him."

"Good plan, Batgirl," I said. If there were a bunch of us and a crowd of them, it would seem natural that I was there.

I spent the rest of the afternoon in school lost in my memories of Italy. Snogging on the Ponte Vecchio. Snogging in the courtyard at the hotel. Snogging at the back of the car park. Oh . . . and yes, all the churches and art and culture as well.

I couldn't wait for school to finish so I could see Jay. I just hoped that my stomach would have stopped gurgling by then.

## The Gurgle Wurgle Song by Izzie

Okay tummy, let's get this straight
We're gonna have a talk about something you'll hate
I'm cutting down the calories, got to lose me some weight
Gonna take me some action before it's too late.

I'm going on a diet and this time it's for real
And I don't give a toss about the way you feel
You can rumble, you can grumble, you can growl,
you can gripe
You can beat out jungle rhythms all through the night
You can gurgle, you can sclurch, you can groan,
you can moan
You can mumble, you can murmur when I'm walking
my way home
You can schurgle your displeasure when I'm out with
my friends
But there's only gonna be one way that this story ends
I'm in this to win. I'm gonna be slim
I'm in this to win. I'm gonna be slim
I'm in this to win. I'm gonna be slim.

My mind's made up and my lips sealed tight
So please shut up now and give up the fight
I'm cutting down the calories, gotta lose me some weight
Gonna take me some action before it's too late.

# Chapter 4

# Nightmare

The evening had started out brilliantly. Nesta, TJ, and I had arrived early so we'd quickly taken over the Ladies cloakroom in a café on Park Road for the necessary preparations: lip-gloss, hair brushing and a squirt of perfume. I put on a double squirt to distract myself from the gorgeous smell of baking that was permeating the café. It was making me feel ravenous.

Chris, Liam, and Eddie had arrived soon after and it was a great reunion as Liam had his photos of the Italian trip as well. Mainly pictures of the boys, larking about. The ones showing Liam were particularly unflattering because someone

(Chris, but Liam doesn't know that) had shaved off one of Liam's eyebrows when he was asleep one night.

After about ten minutes, the café door opened and Jay walked in. I felt my stomach do a back flip. He looked even better than I remembered. In Italy, everything had seemed unreal and there was so much to take in—but seeing him back on our own turf, with his silky black hair and deep brown eyes, I realized he really did stand out in a crowd. He looked taken aback to see me but soon recovered and came over and gave me a big hug like he was pleased to see me. We looked at my pics (I'd taken out any offending ones) and had a laugh as we relived some of the great things we'd all got up to. After about twenty minutes, he started checking his watch and looking awkward. He suddenly stood up and said he had to go. I wondered if I'd said something to offend him. He gave no explanation as to where he was going. And he didn't ask for my number. Or give me his. I felt confused because the chemistry was definitely still there, no doubt about that.

Nesta had been in the Ladies (reapplying her

lip-gloss, no doubt) when Jay left so when she came back, she looked round for him.

"Where's the Bollywood sex god?" she asked.

I shrugged and tried to look cool as I took a sip of my hot water and lemon but I noticed that Liam, Chris, and Eddie exchanged uncomfortable glances. Nesta noticed it too and in her usual subtle way, plunged straight in.

"Okay. What's the story?" she asked.

The boys looked at each other sheepishly and said nothing but Nesta wasn't about to give up.

"Something's going on," she said as she grabbed Eddie's wrist and began to give him a Chinese burn. "Spill or I kill."

"Oww," said Eddie. "Get off! You're hurting me."

"You might as well tell them," said Liam. "They'll find out soon enough . . ."

Nesta let go of Eddie's wrist and he gasped with relief.

"What?" she asked. "What's the mystery?"

Eddie looked at the floor. "Jay has a girlfriend."

"I know," said Nesta. "Izzie."

"No, another girlfriend," said Chris. "Tawny. He's been going out with her for almost a year now."

TJ gasped and glanced over at me anxiously. I felt like someone had punched me in the stomach. A *girlfriend?* It couldn't be true.

Nesta looked angry. "Where's he gone?" she asked as she stood up, rooted out a few pound coins from her pocket and tossed them on the table. "Here. This should cover our share. Two hot chocolates and one lemon water."

TJ and I got up to follow her out. I felt like I was in a trance. This couldn't be happening. As we got outside the café, I ran over the road to the Clocktower as I needed some time on my own.

Nesta and TJ ran after me and Nesta put her arm round me.

I felt like I'd been winded. "*Girlfriend?*" I gasped as I tried to catch my breath. "I can't believe it. He would have told me. Are you sure they meant Jay?"

"Stay cool," whispered Nesta as we saw the boys come out of the café and look for us. "Don't let them see that you're upset."

My heart was sinking as I realized the implications. "They must have all known," I groaned. "This is a total nightmare. What a creep. All that time Jay and I were gazing into each other's eyes and snogging our faces off and he had a girlfriend back here. Chris, Liam, and Eddie must have been having a right laugh. They all knew Jay had someone back here. And she has such a cool name. She's probably gorgeous. Oh God. I hate him. How could he have not told me? It's too awful. I feel such an idiot."

I wanted to go home, curl up under my duvet, and die.

TJ put her arm round me as well. "I'm sure there's some explanation."

"Like what?" I groaned. "Like I was nothing more than a holiday fling?"

"Who knows," said Nesta. "But I'll find out."

"No, please Nesta, leave it," I said as I pulled her back. "I just want to go home."

The girls did their best to persuade me to let them accompany me home but I wanted to be on my own to lick my wounds in private. On the bus home, I gazed out of the window into the gloom. A cold, dark night in February. That was how I felt, cold and dark, like all the color and sunshine had gone out of my world. I wished I hadn't been to Italy. Suddenly all the good memories of my time there seemed like a sham and I

49

felt like binning the photos. Or burning them.

Why hadn't he told me? I kept asking myself. We'd talked so much about our previous relationships and what we wanted. I'd told him all about my exes, not that there were many that counted. Mark, who never called when he said he would, Ben (from the band I sing with who's still a mate) and bad boy Josh who turned out to be a liar. Jay had told me about a girl called Sushila and another called Megan. Nothing about anyone called Tawny though. Nothing about a *steady* girl-friend in his life.

I'd thought I could trust him. You gullible fool, Izzie, I said to myself as I got home, let myself in, and raced up the stairs. I threw myself on my bed and waited for the tears to come. But they didn't. I felt numb. And . . . *hungry*.

I went to the bathroom for a quick weigh in. I must surely have lost a few pounds after today, but no, my weight was the same as in the morning.

Now what? I thought as I went back to my room. What have I got to look forward to? Another freaking grapefruit and if I push the boat out, a piece of soggy lettuce. Maybe that's why he messed me around. I was just some fat bird he met on holiday. Okay for a week but not for a steady relationship. I felt so depressed. I don't care anymore, I thought as I headed for the kitchen. Need chocolate. And need it now.

Ten minutes later, Mum caught me with my hand in the cookie jar.

"I thought you were off those this week," she said as she filled the kettle with water.

"I'm on a new diet," I said as I pushed a chocolate chip cookie into my mouth. "The seafood diet."

"What? Fish?"

"No, I see food and I eat it."

Mum laughed. "Well, at least you haven't lost your sense of humor."

Suddenly, I felt my eyes fill with tears and the cookie felt dry in my mouth.

"What is it, love?" Mum asked.

"Nothing," I said. "Just . . . I hate myself."

Mum looked aghast. "But why?"

"Look at me," I groaned. "I'm supposed to be on a diet and yet here I am stuffing my face. I'm soooo pathetic. No wonder . . ."

"No, love. No. Here, sit down. I'll make us a nice cup of tea and you can tell me all about it. What is it? No wonder what?"

I'd been about to say no wonder boys don't stay with me. How could I tell her what a fool Jay had made of me?

"Don't know . . ." I sighed. "Just . . . why do I always pick the wrong boys? Like, do I have a sign on my forehead that reads "sucker"? I must be doing something wrong or putting out the wrong signals or maybe it's because I'm a great ugly lump and can only attract boys who mess girls' heads up."

Mum took a deep breath. "You're not an ugly lump, Izzie. You're a very pretty girl."

"You have to say that. You're my mum. It comes in the contract you signed at my birth."

I indicated the biscuit and cake wrappers on the table. "But look at me. I don't know what's come over me this week. I wanted to lose some weight but I have *no* will-power."

"Yes you have," said Mum. "What have you eaten today?"

"Before now, two grapefruit and a boiled egg."

"Oh, Izzie," Mum said with a sigh. "You've just been going about losing weight the wrong way. You don't put weight on overnight, although sometimes it appears that way. It creeps on . . ."

"Tell me about it."

"And in the same way, it's not going to come off overnight or in three days. It has to be a more long term process. You still need to eat. That's why you're here stuffing yourself. Not because you're pathetic but because you're hungry and it's perfectly natural."

"So what can I do Mum? I really am serious about wanting to lose a bit. Half a stone, at least."

"Okay," said Mum. "Okay. I'll help. I just want you to promise me one thing and that is that you do it slowly and sensibly with no more thoughts about crash diets. A program of healthy eating and the weight will be off in a few months."

A few *months*? I didn't have that kind of time to waste with the TV pilot coming up. I knew she was probably right. Eat the right kind of foods, etc., etc. but there had to be a quicker way. I still thought I needed to do something drastic at the beginning.

"And do you want to tell me why you think

you attract the wrong boys?" she asked. "What's been going on?"

I shook my head. "Nothing," I said. I felt tired and had done enough caring sharing for one night. Sometimes with parents, you give them an inch and they want a mile. You tell them a little about what's going on in your head and they want the whole package. I could see that Mum was settling in for a heart to heart. And what I needed was a head-to-pillow.

"Night, Mum," I said as I got up. "And thanks."

Mum looked slightly bewildered. "Anytime, Izzie. You do know that, don't you? You can talk to me about anything, anytime."

I nodded. I knew I could. But I couldn't. Not yet. It was all too raw. Maybe later when I'd come through the other side. When I was slim and gorgeous and the boys were queuing up to date me. Maybe then.

Late night weigh-in: the same, the same, the same. Makes no sense to me. I starve, nothing changes. I stuff my face with biscuits, nothing changes.

The seafood diet: See food and you eat it.

# Auditions

"Quite clearly all those stupid diet magazines that say that you can lose ten pounds in a week or two are wrong," I said to Lucy as I came out of the bathroom at her house after school the next day. I'd just been on their scales in there and my weight still hadn't shifted an ounce. And that was after four days of starvation (apart from the odd choc/cookie binge). "The only way to lose ten pounds in a week is to chop one of your legs off."

"I'm sure Lal will help you with that," said Lucy as we went into her room to join Nesta and TJ. "Just go and lie on the kitchen table and I'll get him to get the electric saw from the shed."

I lay back on her bed and pushed my stomach out so that she could see how bad things were. "You don't think I'm serious do you?" I asked.

"Looking like that? No," she replied. "I mean, who goes round deliberately pushing their stomach out? And I've told you before, I think you're mad and I don't want to talk about it anymore."

"Ooh, get you," I said. "Don't want to discuss it."

TJ lay on the floor and like me, tried to push her stomach out as far as it would go. "See," she said, "anyone has a stomach if they push it out far enough."

Nesta looked down at us with disdain from the bed. "Much as I would like to join in the fat tum competition, we have better things to do. Come on. We have to be at the studio in Camden at six."

I was in two minds as to whether to go, even though Mum had finally given me permission as long as I didn't fall behind with my homework. I was still worried about the camera putting another ten pounds on me and felt like I wanted to get myself in shape before I went public again. They're not filming tonight so maybe I'll just go along to check it out then back out later, I thought.

Nesta pulled a couple of outfits out of her ruck-sack. "Now. The question is, what look should I go for?" she asked. "Intellectual with a wonderbra or slut bitch with a brain?"

TJ laughed. "Sounds like the same thing to me. Just go as you are. You're only going to be in the audience and they probably don't want anyone who attracts too much attention."

"Ah, but you've forgotten, they're going to pick a few people for the panel."

"In that case, Nesta," I said, "don't wear anything too revealing. You look good as you are and going with your chesty bits on display might give the wrong impression for the show. Are you sure you're not going to come, TJ?"

TJ shook her head. "Nope. I am here merely in the role of slave and dresser. When you've gone, I'm going to go home, walk Mojo, then get down to some work on the magazine. Now, who needs zipping up?"

In the end, Nesta settled for a black mini, black polo neck, and black knee-high boots. She looked fab. Lucy wore one of the little halter-necks she'd made herself and her black jeans. She looked fab too. I wore a baggy T-shirt and my baggy jeans as those are the only clothes that fit me at the moment. I looked like an old sack.

When we got to the studio, I instantly wished I'd made more of an effort.

"Ohmygod," I said as I took in the crowd shivering in the cold outside the reception building at the studio where the auditions were to be held. There were some really cute boys there and most of the girls were dressed up to the nines and in skimpy outfits despite the weather. In my oversized padded jacket, gloves, and scarf, I felt like a frump compared to those who were in tiny tops and miniskirts and were made up to the eye balls. It was lip-gloss city.

At six on the dot, a blonde girl in glasses opened the door and directed us all into a room where we all had to sign in, give our details, and be given a number and a visitor's pass. Some people were turned away right there and then.

"Too old or too young," said Lucy as one tiny girl who looked about eleven burst into tears as she was asked to leave.

When the remaining teens had signed in, we were ushered down a maze of corridors and into a small cozy studio that smelled of new carpets. In fact, everywhere *was* carpeted (even the walls!) and there was no natural light. It was like walking into a softly-lit cocoon and it was warm so I could take off my jacket. At the front was a stage, on the ceiling were endless wires and lights, and dotted around the sides were a few cameras. It was my first time in a real studio and I felt really excited to be there. There was a buzz of anticipation in the air as everyone talked and eyed each other up.

"Eyes left, over in the corner," said Lucy as a tall boy with dark spiky hair came in from behind the stage and began to fiddle with a microphone in the centre. He was very good looking but more than that, he had a nice face, open and friendly.

"Ding dong. Well fit," I said as we stood in the aisle and looked for the best place to sit. "Now *there's* a way to get over Jay. I wonder if he's attached? Oh . . . but you saw him first, Lucy."

"All yours," she said. "I'm having a break for boys for a while."

"Yeah, right," said Nesta. "Tony's a boy?"

"Yeah. And I told you. We're going to be friends. I said I'd hang out with him every now and then. You know, see a movie . . ."

Nesta laughed. "I have to hand it to him. His technique is faultless."

"What do you mean?" asked Lucy.

"I told you before. He's wheedling his way back in. I don't think you can be just friends with a boy. Not one you fancy, anyway."

Lucy stuck her bottom lip out. "Well I'm not going to cut him out of my life. Why should I when we still like each other?"

"See! I knew this would happen," said Nesta. "Your resistance is weakening day by day. Just friends! Hah. I smell trouble. It will be fine until one of you gets involved with someone else and then . . ."

"But I'm not going to get involved with someone else. Not at the moment. As I said, I'm taking a break."

"Yeah," said Nesta. "Sounds like it."

As they chatted away, I watched the boy with spiky hair working on the stage. There was something about him that was different from the majority of boys in the studio. Maybe it was because he seemed older, maybe about eighteen, whereas the other boys looked about the same age as me. That's it, I thought. That's what I need. Someone more mature. And someone tall so that I don't tower over him like I do most of the boys my age who only come up to my shoulders. Yes. I want someone who's lived a bit and had a few relationships. Maybe they'll be a bit clearer about what they want. Then I thought about Tony and Lucy. He was eighteen and had made it very clear what he wanted. Sex. At that moment, the boy on the stage looked over to where I was standing and we made eye contact. I quickly looked down. I didn't want him to notice me when I was dressed so drably. If we got picked to be in the audience for the run-through on Saturday, I would make more of an effort and turn up in something more attractive.

At the front, a group of boys were shoving each other to get seats directly in front of the stage. I made my way straight for the back row. I knew exactly where I wanted to sit, and that was nowhere near the cameras, even though I knew they weren't filming this time. Not until I was slimmer. Lucy came with me but Nesta went straight down to the stage and found a place on the front row.

After a short while, a couple of men came in and the room grew quiet. One of them looked old, at least fifty, with short gray hair and the other had a shaven head and protruding belly and looked more like a bricklayer than a TV producer. The older one looked round then took a seat at the back near me. The other one went to the microphone that Spiky-Haired Boy had set up.

"Hi," he said. "My name's John Maclean. And I'm one of the producers on the show which, as you probably all know, is going to be called *Teen Talk*. So that we're all on the same page and you know what to expect, I'd like to tell you what the format is going to be. Half an hour with a break for commercials, so we'll run to about twenty-three minutes. First part, topic, nine-minute discussion, guest band. Second part, new topic, nine-minute discussion, then if we have time, we'll have the guest band again and wrap up. So you see, it's going to be tight with not a lot of time for messing around, for people who hog the microphone, for people with a chip on their shoulder or an axe to grind. If the pilot's a goer, we'll do six shows back to back in the autumn so we'll need commitment from you and permission from your parents for you to take part. Consent forms will be given out on the way out. Any questions?"

Nesta was straight in. "What sort of topics will be up for discussion?"

"Our writers are working on that now but any suggestions from the audience will make their job easier. That's why you guys are here. To give us input."

A pretty redhead in the second row put her hand up. "What time will we need to be here?"

"Saturday morning, an hour before kick-off so that will be ten o'clock for you. We want everyone in their place, settled, sorted."

"Will it be live this Saturday?" asked the redhead.

John shook his head. "There will be cameras here but no, it will be a run-through so that we can iron out any hiccups in the early stages."

"Do we get paid?" asked a boy at the back.

"No," John replied. "You won't get paid. You do it for the street cred. Right?"

A few boys from the front groaned then got up and sloped towards the door.

"Street cred?" said one. "You must be joking."

"Yeah. Street cred don't buy yer fags," another called as they went out.

John watched them go with a look of indifference. "Anyone else want to leave?"

"Have you picked the people for the panel yet?" asked a blond boy from the front.

"We'll do that this Saturday. Tonight's just a short meet. Let us meet you, let you know what will be happening. So. Any ideas for topics?"

"Is there a God?" someone called from the back.

"Terrorism," suggested another.

"Politics."

Ideas began flying about. After a while, John put his hand up. "Okay, good. All good ideas but what about stuff that's relevant to you as teenagers?"

"Sex," said one of the boys at the front, and everyone laughed.

"Not having sex," said a girl behind him, and everyone laughed again.

"What do girls want?" suggested another boy.

"What do *boys* want?" said a girl.

I could see that the program was going to be great fun. I wanted to be part of it, so when we were all invited to come back on the Saturday, I decided that I didn't want to use my weight gain as an excuse to hide away. I'd miss out on what was happening. There's only one thing for it, I resolved for the umpteenth time that week. I have to lose weight so I have to be really strict with myself, and no stupid weak moments where I stuff my face with chocolate or anything else.

The only way to lose ten pounds in two weeks, and keep it off, is to chop off your leg.

Chapter 6

# Conspiracy

Channel One: Superchef Delia concocting something delicious with raspberries, ricotta cheese, and cream. Argh.

Change channels.

Channel Two: Nigella, the Domestic Goddess making ice cream out of Mars bars. Mmmmm. I felt my mouth water.

Change channels.

Channel Three: Jamie Oliver and some other celeb chef making lasagne with garlic and herbs in record time. It looked so good, I could almost smell it.

Change channels.

Channel Four: a movie. Phew . . . safe. A movie about an Italian family. I let it run for ten minutes. Oh no, all they do in this film is eat. Pasta, pizza, tiramisu. My stomach is rumbling like crazy.

Change channels.

Channel Five: Commercials. For Maltesers. Thai food. Mexican food like Mama used to make. Cheeseburgers. Slaver, slaver. I'm so hungry, I could lick the screen. Then up comes a commercial for toothpaste. I'm so starving I could even eat some of that. All I've had today was a bowl of cereal (on Mum's insistence), and couple of rice cakes and an orange at lunch-time. No, relax, Izzie, I told myself, think about something else besides food. Another movie is starting. Must be safer than the Italian one. The credits start to roll. A French scene. A street. The title of the movie: *Chocolat*.

!!!

I give up, I thought as I flicked the TV off.

I'd popped in to see Dad on my way home from the studio and while he and Anna put Tom to bed, I'd decided to watch TV. (Anna is Dad's wife, my stepmum, and Tom is my stepbrother. He's four and absolutely gorgeous.) Big mistake, I thought as

I flopped back on their sofa and waited for them to come down. It's hard trying not to eat. It's not the same as giving up cigarettes or alcohol (not that I do either). You need food to live and if you don't give your body any, it objects. And everywhere there are wonderful smells to tempt you. I don't think I'd ever noticed before this week how great food smells: toast wafting in the kitchen in the morning, freshly baked bread coming out of the bakery on the way to school, spices and garlic from Indian and Thai restaurants on the high street when I walked home from school. All calling, beckoning, Izzie, Izzie, eat, eat . . .

"Iz," Anna called from the hall. "I'm ordering takeaway. What would you like? Your usual? Veg curry, rice, chapati?"

I was tempted. Very tempted. But then I thought about the boy with spiky hair at the studio. I wanted to make a good impression and that meant getting back into my old jeans. By Saturday (which meant near starvation).

"Nothing for me," I called back. "I am on a diet."

"Oh no you're not," Dad said, grinning as he came into the living room. "Your mum phoned.

Told me all about this latest nonsense and gave me instructions that Izzie must eat. Oh ja. Or else ve make her eat."

The world is conspiring against me, I thought. First the smells, then the TV, then my mother, then my father. It's no wonder I'm as fat as a pig.

Anna came in to join us and sat on the sofa next to me. "What on Earth are you dieting for?"

"To lose weight of course."

"Pff," she said. "You don't need to do that. You're lovely as you are."

Anna, of course, like just about every female I know, is thin as a rake. At least she is now. She was a bit chubby for a while after Tom was born, but soon lost it.

"How did you lose the weight you put on when you were pregnant?" I asked in the hope that she'd reveal some great secret that I had yet to read about.

"Breast feeding, lack of sleep, and a small son to chase after all day," she replied. "No time to think about food."

Dad stuck his tummy out the way I had earlier this evening. "Diet, huh? If anyone needs to go on a diet around here, it's me."

I wasn't going to argue. He's not exactly fat. More round. Cuddly, especially round the middle, although it suits him. I remember when he and Mum split up and he lost a lot of weight and looked gaunt for a while. I much prefer him this way, looking chubbier but happy.

Anna giggled and pulled her honey-colored hair back into a scrunchy as he strutted round the room with his tummy sticking out.

"All that beer," she said as he sat next to her and she gave his tummy a stroke.

"Beer," he said. "And genes. I'm prone to putting on weight if I'm not careful. So was my dad. So was my granddad. It's in the family. Genes."

"*Noooooo*," I groaned. What hope was there for me? Everyone always says that I take after my dad more than my mum.

"Still at least I've still got my hair," said Dad with a grin, as he ran his fingers through his thick mane of dark hair. "Us Foster men never were baldies. So. What's it to be, girls? Indian or Chinese?"

"Haven't you got any salad stuff or fruit or something?" I asked.

Dad grinned. "Er . . . there might be a lemon in the fridge."

I should have known better than to ask. He and Anna are hopeless when it comes to stocking up on food. They might both be dead brainy (Dad works as a lecturer in English literature at a university in town and Anna is doing a PhD in medieval poetry) but they haven't a clue when it comes to eating properly. They live off takeaways. Normally I don't mind a bit, in fact I enjoy going round there for a curry night but tonight I wanted to eat something without too many calories. What could I do to keep Mum and Dad happy but not break my diet?

"Okay, I'll have a prawn curry," I said. "And I'll scrape the sauce off."

"Mad." Dad sighed as he got up to phone our order through. "Totally bonkers."

By the time the takeaway arrived an hour later, I thought I was going to pass out with hunger. It smelled divine. Spicy and inviting. When Dad offered me some of his spinach paneer and his naan bread, I gave in. And scrape the sauce of my prawn curry? You must be joking. I wolfed the lot and the bits of Anna's that she couldn't finish.

Hopeless, hopeless, hopeless, I told myself when Dad dropped me home later.

For a brief second, I thought about going up to the bathroom and putting my fingers down my throat. Loads of girls at our school do it. Bulimia. Kayley Morrison in our year does it. I've heard her throwing up in the cloakroom after lunch. It's weird. She eats a good lunch. I've seen her. Big sandwiches and chocolate bars. Milkshakes. Then she goes and vomits it all up. Okay, she is slim but she doesn't look good. Her skin looks powdery and she looks unwell somehow. We had a health adviser come in and talk to us about it once. Apparently all the acid regenerated from your stomach rots your teeth. And I didn't fancy being slim and toothless. Not a good look in my book.

I may be desperate but I'm not *that* desperate, I thought as I went in to say hi to Mum and Angus. I shall just cut back tomorrow. If you add everything up that I've eaten so far this week, it must surely be less than I normally eat.

Upstairs, later, I decided to pick out an outfit for

Saturday. There must be something that will look good, I thought as I searched through my wardrobe. A lot of my clothes are black so that's good as it's a slimming color. But everything looked that little bit too tight. T-shirts that had fitted perfectly only months ago stretched unattractively over my boobs, and there was a welt of flab over the top of my jeans.

Maybe I won't bother going on Saturday, I thought. Maybe Mum's right and losing weight is going to be a long-term thing.

My phone bleeped. It was a text message from Dad.

DIET RELIGIOUSLY, it said. EAT WHAT YOU LIKE AND PRAY THAT IT DOESN'T SHOW.

Haha. Not.

Diet religiously: Eat what you like
and pray it doesn't show.

# Chapter 7

# Shopping For Fat Clothes

Weigh-in. Friday morning: I have dropped two pounds. Bizarre. I don't get it. Starve and nothing comes off. Eat a big curry and I lose two pounds. Maybe it was all my efforts to eat little during the day. Whatever. Two down, only six to go. V. v. happy.

"Oh, don't be ridiculous," said Lucy when I told the girls that I was having second thoughts about going tomorrow. "That's such a cop-out."

"I haven't got anything to wear."

"Have you got any money left over from the

Italian trip?" asked Nesta. "You hardly spent a bean, you were too busy snogging Jay to go shopping." She clamped her hand over her mouth. "Oh, sorry. Didn't mean to . . ."

"It's Okay," I said. "You can say his name."

"How much have you got?" asked Lucy.

I did a quick calculation in my head. With this week's pocket money and the money left over from Italy, I'd had fifty, but I'd spent some of it on slimming magazines. "About forty pounds."

"Right. So we go shopping after school and sort you out some new clothes," said Lucy. "I'll be your personal fashion adviser."

"No. I have to lose six pounds first."

Nesta laughed. "Only six? Listen, girl, we're going to help you lose forty."

The mall was heaving when we got there after school. It seemed like half the teen population of North London had had the same idea and the shops were busy, busy, busy. Outside it was wet and windy so it was good to get off the bus and into the dry where we could walk about without getting soaked and our hair wrecked.

After trawling around for the best part of an hour, I still hadn't found anything. Nesta, on the other hand, had found a gorgeous little turquoise silk camisole in Monsoon. Lucy had bought a dinky beaded handbag in Accessorize and even TJ had found something she liked, a strappy olive green T-shirt in TopShop that looked great with her brown hair and eyes.

"Why is it that when you go looking for something," I asked, "you never find it? And when you're not looking, you see all sorts of things?"

"Same with boys," said Nesta. "Go looking and all you meet are geeks. Give up and along comes Mr. Right."

"Or Mr. Right Now in your case," Lucy said, laughing.

Nesta punched her. "Someday my prince will come."

"That's what the girl who left a film to be developed at the photo shop said," Lucy told us. "Some days my prints will come."

Nesta patted her on the head. "Sad," she said. "Very sad."

I tried all my usual shops but nothing looked

right. After an hour, I was ready to give up and become a nun.

"Coffee break," said Nesta. "We need to regroup and reenergize."

"Whatever," I said. Usually I looked forward to our café breaks but today the prospect didn't hold the same allure.

"Come on," said Nesta and led us up the escalator to the floor where all the cafés were.

"I could always make you something, Iz," said Lucy as we stood in the queue to get served.

"By tomorrow? I don't think so."

I felt depressed. And the last shop we'd been into had been the final straw. I had eventually seen an electric blue top that I liked and went to try it on. In the changing room, there were mirrors that showed you from every angle. Front, side, and back. It was horrible. I liked the top but my usual size (twelve) was way too small. I had definitely gone up a size and the thought of being a fourteen filled me with dismay. When I'd shamefully gone out to ask for the bigger size, the snooty assistant had told me that they hadn't got it in "the larger sizes."

"Perhaps I should shop in one of the shops for large ladies," I said when we'd got our drinks (chocolate milkshakes for TJ, Nesta, and Lucy and tea without milk for me) and we sat down.

"Izzie, you *have* to get over this," said Lucy. "You are by no means a large lady. It's getting boring."

"Pff," I said. "Nesta is the only one of you honest enough to say that I'm fat."

Nesta almost spat her milkshake out. "I never did. I *never* said fat."

"Did."

"Didn't."

"Did."

"Did *not*."

"Rivetting conversation," said TJ. "Remind me to hang out with you guys again."

Nesta ignored her. "Did not. Did not. Did not a million times. I said that you had gained a little weight in Italy. You did. A little. But you can carry it. You're five foot eight or whatever."

"Yeah," said TJ. "You're probably exactly the right weight for your height."

"The only way I'd be the right weight for my

height is if I was eight foot seven. I don't want to carry it. I want to be sylph-like. Tall and willowy. I won't be happy until I am."

"Then you'll never be happy," said Nesta. "You are not a sylph-like build. Or willowy. You are, as we've said before, curvy. I really don't know what your problem is. Boys like curves."

"Not as much as they like skinny girls," I protested. "Little girly girls."

"Not what Lal and Steve say," said Lucy. "They say that they like girls that look female, that is, curvy. You're lucky you look the way you do."

"You're just saying that."

"No, I'm not," said Nesta. "I mean, why would you want to be Olive Oyle when you could look like Jessica Rabbit?"

"I saw this program about body image on telly the other night," said TJ. "It was the top-ten things that make a naked body attractive and sexy. Want to know what number one was?"

"Flat stomach," I said.

"Nope."

"Great boobs," said Nesta.

"Nope," said TJ. "And it was something for men

82

*and* women. Great boobs wouldn't look so great on a bloke."

"Three nipples," said Lucy. "And the ability to lick your eyebrows as a party trick?"

"Yeah, right," TJ said, laughing. "No. It was confidence. All the experts said the same. Whatever shape or size, if you're confident, it is a million times more attractive than trying to hide your body or make excuses for some of it."

"That's what Lal says," said Lucy. "He said he can't stand these girls who are always going on about the size of their bum. He said that what girls don't realize is that most boys are happy that girls have got bums, whatever the shape."

"He would," said Nesta. "But it makes sense. Confidence. Yeah. Strut your stuff and if you've got it, flaunt it."

Easier said than done, I thought. I can't imagine strutting my stuff, naked or clothed.

"So, Iz. You've got to chill," said Nesta. "You look great. So you've gone up a size. Big deal. We're teenagers. We're bound to be growing."

"But not in every direction."

"Nobody's totally happy about the way they

look," said Lucy. "Even some of the top models hate certain aspects of their bodies."

"Yeah. Get off this trip, Izzie. We all have hang-ups," said Nesta. "Like me and my stupid big feet. Size nine. I hate them. But I can't do anything about it unless I chop my toes off. And this stupid brace I have to wear. Do you think I like that? No way. Some days I think that all people see when they look at me is a metalmouth."

"And I hate being mini me," said Lucy. "Don't you think I'd like to be taller? And have boobs. How do you think I feel hanging out with you three? Sometimes I think I look like I'm traipsing after my big sisters."

"And I hate my shape," said TJ. "Straight, up down. No waist. At least you have a waist, Izzie."

"And boobs," said Lucy.

"And nice feet and great teeth," said Nesta.

"And beautiful eyes," said TJ. *"Bella ochi."*

I could see I wasn't going to get any sympathy here as they all went into a mock sobbing act.

"Oh, I'm so ugly," wailed Nesta.

"And I'm uglier," TJ joined in.

"And *I'm* the ugliest of all," cried Lucy.

A couple of boys went past and looked at us as though we were all barking mad and that set us off laughing.

"Seriously though, Iz," said TJ. "If you're really worried about having gained a few pounds, we're here to help. Aren't we guys?" She looked at Nesta and Lucy.

"Yeah. We'll give you advice," said Lucy, then grinned mischievously. "Like want to diet? Go to the paint store—you can get thinner there."

I laughed then punched her. "Oh, very funny. Not."

"And I know a great way to lose weight," said Nesta. "Eat naked in front of a mirror. Restaurants will almost always throw you out before you can eat too much."

I rolled my eyes. "You lot aren't taking me seriously."

"We would if you had a genuine problem," said TJ. "But you don't, you really don't. Okay, so you don't look like a stick-thin model out of a magazine but neither do they half the time. Did you know that they can airbrush them to look that way?"

"Be great if you could do that in real life," I said. "Someone would make a fortune."

"It's all about dressing for your particular body shape," said Lucy. "I can help with that."

"What? By advising me to cover up in a baggy top?"

"Most definitely not," said Lucy. "Baggy clothes can make people look bigger. You need to show off your shape, not hide it."

"And if you want to lose a few pounds," said TJ, "exercise. That will burn off a few calories."

"And in the meantime, let's talk about something more interesting," said Nesta. "Like that group of lads at the table over there. They've been eyeing us up since we sat down. Now, can we be bothered with them or shall we resume our shopping?"

We all did the room scan the way that Nesta had taught us, i.e.: don't look directly at boys in question, instead look around the whole room in a general sweep taking in the boys as you do. That way, you appear to be cool and not desperate and on the look out.

"No thanks," I said when I'd done the "sweep." There was no one there I fancied. They looked about our age. Too young. And short.

As we finished our drinks, I made a mental note to lighten up. Even though I felt that the girls were only saying that I looked okay to make me feel better, I could see that I was in danger of becoming a real bore about being big. I resolved to be more fun in future so on the escalator going back down into the mall, I treated them to my impersonation of a cross-eyed robot.

For some reason, they all decided to join in. It was then that I spotted a boy I dated last year. Mark. I quickly darted behind a pillar at the bottom of the escalator. He was the last person I wanted to see. And he was holding hands with a girl. A willowy, thin girl wearing a tiny tank top, which revealed a midriff as flat as a pancake.

So boys prefer curvy girls do they? Yeah right. I felt more determined than ever to drop some weight. I just wouldn't go on about it anymore to the girls.

Number one secret to being attractive:
Confidence.

# Chapter 8

# Knock Out

I started my exercise regime first thing the next morning.

Up down, up down, up down. And now the other eyelid.

After I'd got out of bed, I went into my preparations for the run-through of *Teen Talk*. The girls wouldn't hear of me not going so I'd decided to be positive about it. Today, I wanted to make an impression on Studio Boy and I was determined not to let my weight problem get in the way.

I made a big effort blow-drying my hair, then ran my ceramic irons through it so that it was dead straight. Then I tried on some of the clothes in my wardrobe. First, my black jeans and I found that they were a tad looser than they had been on Monday. Hurrah. If I held my breath, I could get away with wearing them. I could wear a little camisole on top and a jacket over it. If I kept the jacket on, then no one would notice the wodge of splodge hanging over my waistband. Final touches were my amethyst earrings, purple bead choker, a slick of lip-gloss, a squirt of the Jo Malone Tuberose perfume that my stepsister, Amelia, had given me for my last birthday, and I was ready to go.

After dressing, I went downstairs and had a piece of dry toast for breakfast (as the last thing I wanted was my stomach to start rumbling when we were in the audience). Mum was in a really good mood and happy to see me eating, if only toast. I asked her if I could join the local gym and miracle of miracles, she said it was a great idea and asked me to drop in and check out the joining fees. She said that she had been thinking about getting fitter and that her and Angus might join as well, though Angus went as white as his hair and didn't look too happy about the suggestion at all.

Nesta and Lucy were meeting up in Highgate

and going on the Tube down to Camden but I had taken on board what TJ had said yesterday about exercise and decided to walk there. It was the new, upbeat, "I can do this, I shall exercise myself thin" me. It would take about half an hour if I went at a good pace.

Big mistake.

When I set off, the sky was clear but as I reached Highgate Hill, clouds began to appear. And then more clouds. By the time I reached Kentish Town, the heavens opened and it poured down. I hadn't thought to take an umbrella so I ran as fast as I could and by the time I reached the studio, I was red in the face, my lovely straightened hair was plastered to my cheeks, my mascara had run and I was soaked through.

I was also ten minutes late and the guy on the reception had closed the entrance door.

"Please," I mouthed to him through the glass.

I must have looked such a pathetic sight that he relented and let me in.

"Better move it," he said. "The others went in ages ago."

I raced along the corridor and just as I was

turning into the studio, the door opened and someone came out. Mature boy with the spiky hair and I smacked right into him.

The papers he was carrying went everywhere and as I bent down to help him retrieve them, unfortunately it was at exactly the same time that he did and our heads banged together.

"Ow," he said, coming up fast.

"Ouch," I said, coming up after him.

"You always make this kind of impression on first encounter?" he asked.

"Yeah," I said as I rubbed my head. "I like to knock people out when I meet them."

He sniffed the air near my neck. "Hey, you smell nice."

I smiled. "Jo Malone."

He put out a hand. "Gabriel."

"No," I said. "My name's Izzie. Jo Malone is the maker of the perfume."

"I know. Just joshing," he said, then raised an eyebrow. "Classy stuff. I like her scented candles."

As we talked, I noticed that I was dripping water onto the floor.

"Oh God," I said. "I got caught in the rain. I must look such a mess . . ."

"Not at all." Gabriel smiled. "Just a bit wet that's all. Actually I . . . I noticed you the other day . . ."

"Because I was a mess then too? I felt such a frump when I got here and saw how everyone else looked."

"No. But that's why I noticed you. Not because you looked like a frump at all. Far from it. You looked like a real person. So many of the others had put on all their clubbing clothes, like dressed to impress. I noticed you and thought, she looks like a girl you could actually have a proper conversation with."

Wow, I thought as he opened the studio door for me. A boy who knows his perfumes, likes scented candles and makes you feel good even when you know you look like crapola.

"You'd better go in. And don't worry, they haven't got started yet."

"Thanks," I said as I tiptoed in.

"Catch you later," he said.

Nesta was sitting down near the front with

Lucy and they gave me a wave as an usher directed me to a seat on the back row.

Nothing much was happening yet and for the next forty minutes or so, everyone in the audience just sat about, chatted and watched as the crew set up lighting and cameras and Gabriel brought in a stool and a guitar and set up a mike in front of them. Rumor had it that the guest on the first show was going to be Alicia Prowdy, an American singer-songwriter. I couldn't wait. I loved her stuff and had one of her CDs at home.

At around eleven, just as I was about to nod off, John (the producer we'd met on Thursday) came in with Geena Parker and everyone sat up in anticipation. I'd seen Geena before on TV. She had the usual teen show presenter looks: long legs, slim, blonde, smiley face. She was one of the celebrities that I'd read about in one of my slimming magazines. She said in the article that it's part of her job to stay in shape and she has to work hard at it as TV can make you look bigger than you are. She said she jogs every day and never drinks alcohol. As she went down to the stage, I wondered if she ever splurged out on chips or chocolate or if she was always strict with herself? She began talking to four teens in the front row and asked them to take their places. Must be the panel, I thought as they made their way onto the stage. There was a tall blond boy, quite cutelooking in the King of the Elves, *Lord of the Rings* kind of way but not my type. Next to him was a pretty brunette with a ponytail who looked very uncomfortable, next to her, a girl with short red hair and a cheeky face who looked like she might be interesting, and beside her at the end, a boy with dark hair and bushy eyebrows.

After a few preliminary instructions from John, the first discussion soon got under way. I was so busy watching what Gabriel was doing that I missed what the topic was.

"What's it about?" I asked the girl sitting next to me.

"Jealousy," she whispered back as the noise level at the front grew.

Geena began roving the stage and the audience. Immediately I could see that she was having a hard time controlling the proceedings as people kept calling out from the audience, talking over each other, shouting, and Mr. Eyebrows was the loudest of them all. He seemed to be doing his best to dominate the whole discussion. •

After about five minutes, John shouted, "Cut."

He went on to the stage and shook his head. "Right. This isn't working, guys," he said. "We have to have some order here. Geena will let you know when she wants you to speak and you lot on the panel, for heaven's sake, give each other a break. Let each other talk or no one's going to get heard." At this point he looked at Eyebrows.

The discussion got underway again as Geena asked, "So . . . jealousy. A green-eyed monster or a healthy emotion? Let's hear what our panel has to say." She looked at the redhead girl to say something.

"It can be difficult if someone's flirty by nature and their partner is insecure," she started, "but I guess it all comes down to trust. I think . . ."

"If you're in a relationship," Eyebrows butted in, "why are you flirting?"

"I didn't say *I* was flirting or that I was in a relationship," said the redhead. "I was about to . . ."

"Jealousy sucks," said Eyebrows. "It's a negative emotion."

The Elfin King on the panel began to try and say something but Eyebrows talked (or rather shouted) over him so he backed down. The red-head looked as though she wanted to sock Eyebrows and the girl with the pony-tail looked like she was going to cry. And then she did.

"Stop shouting," she said then got up and ran off.

Geena looked bewildered for a moment then turned to the audience. "Let's hear from our studio audience. Anyone got anything to say?"

"Cut, cut," called John from the back. "Cue the song."

A few moments later, a stunning tall thin girl with long, dark hair and wearing jeans and cowboy boots got up and began to sing a country and western type ballad. It *was* Alicia Prowdy. She's one of my favorite singer-songwriters as not only do I love her voice but also her image. She's exactly how I'd like to look. I couldn't believe my luck in being there to see her and hear her sing live. The moment didn't last long though because behind me, I could hear Geena and John having a heated discussion about how best to run the show.

"This is a disaster," whispered John. "You have

to take control. Get them to raise their hands."

"Like in school? No way," said Geena. "They're teens, not kids."

"It's not going to work otherwise . . ."

I tried to concentrate on Alicia but it was useless with them bickering behind me and just as they stopped, the song finished and John announced that we were having a break.

The noise level grew as everyone started chatting and Lucy crept up to sit with me. "Think I'll stay back here from now on," she said. "I thought it was going to end up in fisticuffs down there."

After about ten minutes, John went back down to the stage.

"We're going to try again," he said then pointed at Nesta. "You, second row. Want to try out for the panel?"

Nesta nodded, quickly took her place on the stage then looked to find Lucy and me at the back. We gave her the thumbs-up.

"You," said John pointing at Eyebrows, "thanks a lot and we'll get back to you. For the moment, could you sit at the back, and we'll give someone else a go."

Eyebrows looked surprised and got up, but instead of going to the back, he walked out, slamming the door behind him.

John pointed at a small Harry Potter lookalike in the second row. "You. Panel. Let's go again and try to keep it civil this time. If you want to say anything, raise your hand."

As Harry Potter boy took his place on the stage, Geena walked back down to the front and beamed into one of the cameras. "Welcome back to *Teen Talk*. The show where we want to hear what teens are talking. No. Can I do that again? Okay. Welcome to *Teen Talk* where we listen, teens talk. Oh, bugger. I'll do that again. Welcome to *Teen Talk*. The topic for the second part of our show is faithfulness. How important is it in a relationship?"

This time the discussion proceeded more successfully with Geena making it very clear who she wanted to talk and when.

"I believe it's one hundred percent important," said the redhead girl. "Why be in a relationship if you're not going to stick with it?"

"Even if your partner wasn't being faithful?" asked Geena.

Nesta raised her hand and Geena indicated for her to go ahead. "I think if he's being unfaithful, there's no point in having a relationship because the trust can't be there and that's one of the most important things." I got the feeling she was talking about herself and Luke and TJ before Christmas.

"Good point," said Geena. "But sometimes you don't know when someone's being unfaithful."

"Tell me about it," said Nesta, rolling her eyes. Everyone laughed.

"But at our age, how can we know what we want if we don't experiment?" said Elfin King. "And sometimes that means letting someone down."

"Yeah, but what about loyalty? What about commitment?" asked Geena. "In fact is there a difference?"

It was at this moment that I felt a rush of adrenaline and before I had time to think about speaking in front of so many people, I had put my hand up.

"At the back," said Geena. "Dark hair."

"Um . . ." I began as all eyes turned to look at me. "I think there's a huge difference. Loyalty is something you want to do, whereas commitment sounds like something you have to do."

"Explain," said Geena.

"Um . . . commitment is the word used for when people get sent to prison, you know, they get committed. Like there's no choice involved. Loyalty is different. You choose to be loyal to certain people because you care about them. And if you care about someone—whether it's a mate or a boyfriend, then you wouldn't want to hurt them by being unfaithful."

"But what if the relationship isn't working anymore and you meet someone you like better? That will hurt them. Should you tell them?" asked a boy in the row in front of me.

I waited until he had finished, then nodded. "Absolutely. What could be worse than stringing someone along? It might hurt but I think it's better to admit when something isn't working. So what I'd say is that you have to be faithful to the truth."

A couple of girls in the audience clapped and the discussion carried on. I hardly heard anyone for the next few minutes as I couldn't believe that I had managed to get my thoughts out.

After the run-through, Gabriel came over and sat beside me.

"Hey, you were really good," he said. "I liked what you said."

"Thanks. It's weird talking in front of so many people. It's like everything goes into slow motion."

He nodded. "Some people totally lose it in front of a camera. People who are normally coherent go blank or freeze. You seemed completely at ease."

I laughed. "Not how I felt."

"Shame it's only the run-through today as your comments would have made good TV. Still, we have to do it this way so that we can see how it looks and we can get a rough idea of who can talk and who's going to choke before we do the first show. As you can see, we have a few things to iron out but we'll get there."

"But what about Alicia?"

"Oh, her bit will be used. She's only here this week so we had to prerecord her."

"So what do you do here?"

"I'm on work experience from college. I'm doing media studies and want to work in TV. Producing, I think. I'm still not sure. Our tutor fixed it up so that I could work here for a few days a week. My official title is General Dogsbody."

I laughed. "Okay, General."

After that we got chatting and I found him really easy to talk to, like he was one of the gang and as people milled around the studio, we sat there having a laugh and making bitchy comments about what people were wearing and what they'd said. As everyone was getting ready to leave, he put his hand over mine.

"Been great to meet you, Izzie. As I said before when you tried to knock me out, I thought we'd get on the first time I saw you. In fact, you remind me of my sister."

*Sister?* I thought as I got up to go. *Sister!* I really fancied him and had hoped that he felt the same way but I reminded him of his sister? Who'd want to snog their sister? I hoped that he'd ask for my number or ask if we could see each other again but he didn't. Maybe it's because I'm fat, I thought. Maybe he feels safe with me and that's why he can chat away to me. No danger of any complications. I remember when TJ went through something similar. She fancied this boy called Scott but he treated her like a confidant and said he could talk to her as she was like one of the boys. By now, the wonderful high I'd felt earlier had vanished and I felt like a deflated balloon brought down to Earth after losing its air.

One of the boys. A sister. Safe. Dogs' poo, I thought as I joined the others filing out of the studio into the horrible gray afternoon.

Izzie's exercise regime:
Up down, up down.
And now the other eyelid.

# Chapter 9

# Temptation
## Alley

As it had stopped raining when we got out of the studio, we decided to go up to Camden Lock and have a cruise around the market. Nesta was over the moon at having been picked to be on the panel and she wondered why I didn't feel the same high.

"Because Gabriel thinks I'm like his sister," I groaned as we headed up the high street and I filled them in on my conversation with him.

"His sister might be a real hottie," said Nesta. "He might have paid you the most wonderful compliment in the world. What is going on with you lately, Izzie? You're so down on yourself."

"Yeah," said Lucy. "And you're usually Miss Positive."

I shrugged. "Dunno. Just . . . oh, it's just I seem to be losing all my confidence. It's gone down the plughole."

"Why don't you do some of your affirmations?" asked Lucy. "All that full of joy stuff you always used to chant. Remember I am full of joy, I am full of joy, I am full of joy."

"Right. I am full of joy," I said miserably.

Usually I'm a great believer that state of mind is often due to choice. Tell yourself that you're miserable and your mind goes, okay, yeah, I am. Choose to be happy and you can be—and you can boost the feeling by making positive affirmations. But fat? I hadn't chosen that and yet it was the reason for my mood and my loss of confidence. Maybe Lucy was right. I should start doing my affirmations.

"And do one of your visualizations," said Nesta. "Visualize yourself the exact size you want to be, having a great time with Gabriel. Maybe it will come true."

I knew that Nesta thought that visualizations (unless they were of racks of clothes at the mall) were baloney, and she was just trying to be supportive.

"Thanks, Nesta. I will." I tried to imagine myself as she said but couldn't get the image right. I kept seeing myself as the Blob girl surrounded by skinny minnies.

Just as we were going over the bridge on the approach to the Lock, Lucy swerved to the left.

"Let's cross over," she said and tried to hustle us across the road which wasn't a good idea as there was a great double decker bus coming straight at us.

"Woah, what's the hurry?" I asked as I pulled her back on to the pavement.

Lucy looked over my shoulder, then tried to drag me over the road again. She'd clearly seen someone she wanted to avoid so I looked around to see who it might be. About ten metres down the pavement, Jay was coming towards us, hand in hand, with a pretty blonde girl. She was pointing at something in a shop and he was pulling her on. And then he saw us, met my eyes, and froze. He looked away and hauled the girl into the nearest shop.

"Ohmigod!" said Lucy.

"She must be the steady girlfriend," I said. "Tawny."

"What? Who?" asked Nesta, who had missed the whole episode.

"Jay," I said. "He just went into that shop over there with his girlfriend."

"Did he see you?"

"Oh yes. Most definitely."

I felt sick. First Gabriel tells me I remind him of his sister and now Jay appears, as if to remind me that I was just a holiday fling. I felt a negative visualization coming on. Primarily of meeting Jay down an alley and whacking him around the head. With a wet fish.

"Done a runner, has he?" asked Nesta. "Let's follow him in there and see how he handles it. We could offer to show him some photos from the Italian trip, some of him snuggling up to you. Have you got any with you? Yeah. Let's see him worm his way out of that."

She was about to race into the shop after him but I pulled her back.

"No, Nesta, leave it," I said.

"But you can't. I think you should go after him and tell him what you think of him," said Nesta.

"What? When Tawny's with him?"

"She needs to hear what he's like. Tell her how he was two-timing her while he was in Italy."

I shook my head. "No. Leave it."

"I'll go," said Nesta. "What was it you were saying earlier about being faithful to the truth? Now's your chance."

"No. I don't want to cause a scene."

Nesta hurrumphed. "I am *sooo* sick of boys who think they can get away with MURDER," she said at the top of her voice causing a passing punk guy to stop and stare at her. "He had a fab time with you and now he's back with his girlfriend having a merry old time and you've been hurt. It's not fair. You weren't to know that he was in a relationship. I could kill him."

"Yeah, go and kill him," muttered the punk guy before walking on.

"I am full of joy," I chanted. "I am full of joy, full of joy, full of joy."

"I'm not," said Nesta. "I am full of anger, full of anger, full of anger." She kicked a lamppost causing another passerby to stare at her.

"Well, I am full of wee, full of wee, full of wee,"

said Lucy as she began to cross the road again. "I need to find a Ladies."

"Yeah, let's go to the market," I said as I began to follow her. "I need retail therapy."

We walked into the indoor market which was heaving with the usual Saturday Camden crowd: goths, punks, hippies, townies, people of every nationality. Everyone was swarming around looking at the stalls selling everything under the sun: jewelry, clothes, Eastern artifacts, antiques, oils, CDs, cushions—you name it and you can probably find it at the Lock.

After mooching about there for a while, we wandered through to the back of the Lock to see what was going on in the shops under the arches and in the outdoor section.

As we headed out, the delicious aroma of spices, onions, and garlic wafted towards us.

"Oh no," I said. "Temptation alley."

Just outside the indoor market is a maze of corridors with stalls selling every kind of food you can imagine: Thai, Indian, Mexican, Greek, burgers, muffins, bagels.

"Come, eat," called a pretty Thai girl from

behind one stall. In front of her was an array of fabulous-looking exotic dishes.

"Mmm," said Nesta. "I'm starving. Fancy some noodles?"

"Or a burrito," said Lucy, looking at a Mexican stall.

"I'm going to make a run for it," I said, thinking that the faster I was away from there, the better. "I'll see you in Cyberdog."

And with that, I ran down the alley until I was out of the vicinity of all the appetising smells and into another alleyway under the arches that smelt heavily of joss sticks.

"Phew, made it," I said to myself as I had a quick look at a stall selling Indian artifacts and then went on into Cyberdog.

Cyberdog is my favorite shop in London. It's like nowhere else. When you walk in, it's as if you've entered a time capsule in a sci-fi movie. The front of the shop is an open area with a café pounding with music. Through arches at the back are the clothes rails and the assistants who look like they're extras in *Star Trek*.

I gazed in awe at one tall girl whose head was

shaved at the back, with a sprout of dark hair at the top like a black tiara. She was dressed from head to toe in black with silver belts and boots and glasses. She looked like an alien princess.

The clothes were something else, too. They always are in there. Tops with the bottom seams lined with coathanger-type wire so that they stick out from your body. Stunning perspex chokers and bracelets with studs in them that look glamorous and dangerous at the same time. I spied a gorgeous black mesh top with satin ribs sewn up the front and then I saw the outfit that had my name on it. Absolutely perfect *and* it was reduced from fifty-five pounds to thirty. It was a sleeveless top and mini skirt in black pinstripe. Up the centre of the skirt was a silver zip and on the top, from the collarbone to the waist over the boobs were two more silver zips. It looked fabulous. And if I bought it I could wear them separately. I quickly took it off the rail and went to try it on.

As I was in the changing room, I heard Nesta and Lucy calling my name.

"In here," I said and peeked round the curtain.

"Wow," said Lucy as she pulled the curtain aside

so that she could see. "That makes you look amazing. And really slim."

"You have to buy it," said Nesta. "Can you afford it?"

I looked at the price again. With the money I had left from Italy, I could easily do it and have ten pounds over.

I nodded. "Mum's going to hate it but . . . give me a tick and we'll go to the cash desk."

At that moment, Nesta's phone rang. A second later, she handed the phone to me in the changing room.

"Jay," she said as her and Lucy crowded in with me so that they could listen. "He must have got my number from Chris or Liam."

"Is that Izzie?" asked Jay as I took the phone.

"Yes."

"Listen. About earlier . . . I'm so sorry and I want to explain. Can you talk?"

Nesta, who had her ear pressed against my head, pulled a disapproving face.

"Yes. But I haven't got a lot to say."

"That girl you saw me with . . ."

"Yes. Tawny. We . . . I know all about her. Your

steady girlfriend. Funny how you forgot to mention her when we were in Florence."

"I . . . I only didn't mention her because . . . well, it's over . . ."

"Oh. Didn't look that way to me."

Lucy, who had her ear pressed to the other side of my face, gave me the thumbs-up.

"I'm just waiting for the right time to tell her," said Jay.

Nesta feigned a yawn.

"Yeah, right," I said.

"No, really. I still want to see you and I'm sorry that you saw us before I'd got it sorted. Can we meet up?"

"Oh. So you've told her already?"

"No . . . not exactly. But I will. I'm going to."

"Yeah, sure," I said again. "Heard that one before."

And I ended the call and gave Nesta back her phone.

She looked at me in surprise. "That it?"

"That's it."

"You're not going to see him?"

"No way," I said as I picked up my new outfit and headed for the cash desk. "I'm not stupid.

Remember what you went through with Luke? No way am I going there. Someone's either involved with someone else or they're free. I don't do in-betweens."

"That's what's so top about you, Izzie," said Nesta. "You're brilliant. So clear about things. Like the rest of us are all more easily taken in by a bit of smooth talk . . ."

"Speak for yourself," said Lucy. "Your brother's one of the smoothest talkers around and I'm resisting him."

"For the moment," said Nesta. "But he's wearing you down. Anyone can see that . . ."

"Hey, give me some credit," said Lucy. "He's not wearing me down at all. I'm a free agent at the moment and enjoying it, but that doesn't mean to say that I can't see who I want, when I want, and that includes Tony."

"Yeah. Okay," said Nesta, "but before we went to Italy, you were determined that it was all over. End of story. And now, you're seeing him again. I bet Izzie's not going to start seeing Jay again as friends are you, Iz?"

I shook my head. "No way."

"See, you're nobody's fool. You're a wise woman. Smart about what matters."

I could see that Lucy was starting to get annoyed. "And are you saying that I'm not smart because I'm seeing your brother?"

"Yeah," said Nesta.

"But it's different with us," said Lucy. "Tony hasn't been two-timing me. I have no reason to cut him out of my life. We still like each other. Okay, so we want different things right now but that needn't stop us being mates."

"She's right," I said. "Jay has behaved really badly. Tony hasn't."

"Not yet," said Nesta.

"Sometimes, I think that you're jealous," said Lucy. "Jealous that I hang out with him so much."

Nesta shrugged. "Whatever," she said. "I just wish I was as clear about things as Izzie."

"But you are," I said. "You cut Luke out of your life after you'd found out that he was messing you around. So you're nobody's fool either. In fact, I think we're all pretty smart these days when it comes to boys."

"I guess," said Nesta. "Yeah. Okay. So I'm smart

J. Just . . . all I'm saying Lucy, is be careful with Tony. I don't want to see you get hurt."

"I will be," said Lucy. "And you needn't worry. I don't want to get involved with him again. I know he might be leaving in September and once he starts university, he's not going to want some girlfriend back home that he has to answer to. I'm aware of that so I'm not going to set myself up to get hurt."

"But I thought he said he'd go to a university in London so he could be near you," I said.

"He did," said Lucy. "But I also know that he applied to Oxford and if he gets an interview there and they make him an offer, it's going to be hard to resist."

For a moment, she looked sad. She's putting on a brave face about all of this, I thought as I watched her. It must be hard keeping her feelings at bay because she knows it's inevitable that Tony will move on, no matter what he says to her about wanting to stay in London. His life is going to take him in another direction and she's trying really hard to accept that.

I gave her a hug. "I reckon we've all got our

heads well screwed on," I said as the *Star Trek* princess assistant began to pack my outfit. "Shame, though. I did like Jay. He was probably the best-looking boy who's ever shown an interest in me."

"What about Gabriel? He's pretty hot," said Nesta. "Not my type but he's a cutie."

"And I remind him of his sister."

"You won't when he sees you in that new outfit," said Nesta.

"Whatever," said Lucy. "But what does it matter that Jay is good looking or Gabriel? Beauty is only skin deep and anyway it's better to be beautiful on the inside. Like you Izzie."

"Pff," I said. "Born inside out. Just my luck."

Lucy laughed. "No. It's true, Izzie. But you look beautiful on the outside too. Course you do. But one of the things we love about you is that you're clear about what you want, you take no bull from anyone and you *are* wise."

If they knew what really went on in my head, they wouldn't say that, I thought, as I paid for my outfit and we headed back out into the market.

I suppose I can be clear and give advice sometimes, but only to others. I can't do it for myself.

And so here I am, the Wise Woman of Wonga with no boyfriend. Why do I even bother about losing weight and trying to look good when Gabriel, the only boy I fancy at the moment, hasn't even taken my number and Jay, the boy I did fancy, is a two-timing waste of space?

As we strolled along, a bunch of boys cruised past. They looked like they hadn't a care in the world.

"It's not fair, is it?" I said as I watched the boys saunter up to a coffee bar and order drinks.

"What's not?" asked Lucy.

"Looking good," I said. "It's so easy for boys. Us girls, we cleanse, we tone, we exfoliate, we moisturize, we diet, we exercise, we wax, we makeup, and rub lotions and potions into our bodies so that we smell sweet. We agonize over what to wear. And what do boys do. Shave and maybe whack on a bit of hair gel. Huh! That's what I say."

"That's if they do shave," said Nesta. "Some of the ones I know don't even do that yet or only have to do it every other week."

"Huh to boys," said Lucy. "It's true. They don't have to suffer to be beautiful at all, least not in the same way that we do."

As the enticing aromas of temptation alley hit me on the way out, I thought, I'm sick of suffering to be beautiful. To hell with it, Lucy is right about one thing. I do know what I want and the smell is calling me to it. Izzie, Izzieeeeee . . .

Like, who needs boys when you can have burritos?

> "I can resist everything except temptation."
> —Oscar Wilde

# Chapter 10

# The
# X Factor

On the way home, we met up with TJ then stopped off at the gym in Muswell Hill and picked up a brochure and price list for Mum. A girl from the reception showed us around and it did look fab. It had a good-sized pool, two studios offering classes in everything from dance and yoga to Pilates. The gym had all the latest equipment and best of all, there were some fit looking trainers hanging about ready to help anyone in need. I was looking forward to making exercise a part of my plan, since I didn't seem to be able to stick to any of the diets I'd tried for even twenty-four hours. Exercise was the clearly the solution, burn off the extra calories instead of starving then stuffing.

"Poor Angus," I said as we stepped back out into the street after our look round. "Mum wants him to join the gym as well, so there goes his peace and quiet."

"Don't worry," said Nesta. "My dad joined a gym in the new year in a fit of inspiration, but I think he thought that it was all he had to do. Join the gym and bingo, he'd be fit. I think he only ever went once."

"I always liked your dad," I said. "Good man."

"That's not the attitude," said TJ. "If you want to get in shape, you just have to find the type of exercise that you like doing."

"I am in shape," I said. "Round is a shape. And no problem in knowing exactly what I like. Lying on the sofa, watching a good DVD, munching Maltesers."

TJ rolled her eyes. "I give up."

"No. I'm just kidding. I will do it. I'm serious about the exercise thing. Honest."

"Yeah, I may have to join as well," said Nesta.

"Those cute instructors, hubba hubba, ding dong."

"Me too," said Lucy then she sighed. "But then I suppose we'd have to exercise wouldn't we? We couldn't just go along to ogle the guys?"

I was glad that I wasn't the only one who wasn't fitness mad, like TJ. But it did seem unfair that Lucy and Nesta could avoid it and still stay slim.

"Exercise is good for you," said TJ and did a handstand up against a wall. Unfortunately, her jacket and T-shirt slipped down exposing her bra and a boy of about eleven who was walking past almost choked on the ice cream he was eating.

"Cool," he said when she flipped back up onto her feet. "Do that again."

"She's old enough to be your mother, sonny," said Nesta.

"I like older women," said the boy, grinning.

As we walked back up to The Broadway in Muswell Hill and the shops (trying to shake off the boy who tried to follow us in the hope that TJ would do another handstand), I couldn't help but notice that all the boys we passed did a double take when they saw Nesta. When she went into a shop to get some water, I turned to Lucy and TJ.

"Do you ever feel invisible when you're with Nesta?"

Lucy faked shock horror. "Oh, you spoke to me? I didn't realize that I could be seen."

"I'll take that as a yes then?"

"Double yes. It's amazing how people stare at her and never even notice that I'm here too. I could be walking along with my knickers on my head and they wouldn't look when she's around."

"And boys only notice me when I stand upside down," said TJ, "and show the world my bra."

"What are you talking about?" asked Nesta coming back out to join us.

"You," I said. "And the fact that you have amazing pulling power. We were just saying that we feel invisible when we're with you."

"Rubbish. You have pulling power too." She pointed at a group of boys sitting on the other side of the road on the wall outside Ryman's stationery shop. "I'll prove it."

"Prove it? How?" asked TJ.

"Come with me, my little fruitcakes," she said as she led us across the zebra crossing and into the entrance of Sainsbury's supermarket. "Okay," she said. "I'll go first. I'll walk past the boys, then come back, and you have to watch how many of them check me out."

"You don't need to bother," I said. "They all will."

But she was off. And I was right. As she sauntered casually by, they stared at her appreciatively and a couple nudged each other.

A few minutes later, she was back. "Score?"

I counted the boys. Six of them.

"Six out of six," said Lucy.

TJ went next. This time four of the boys gave her the once-over as one seemed to be engrossed on his mobile and another was busy picking his nose.

Next was Lucy and she got the same score. Four out of four as the fifth boy was still talking on his phone and nose picker had started on his other nostril.

"Okay, Iz. Your turn," said Nesta.

I began to walk past the boys but I could see already that they were distracted by some of their mates who'd appeared from inside a café. As I approached them, only one of them checked me out. Doomed to failure, I thought. Invisible. And then I remembered a film I'd seen at Christmas with Judy Garland in it. I couldn't remember what it was called but she was after a part in a show and the producers took her out to see if she had the X factor in public. Just as Nesta was asking us do, the producers made Judy walk down a busy street and they walked behind to see if anyone had noticed her. She did her best to look smiley and sexy but no one was taking the slightest bit of notice. She began to panic. The producers started shaking their heads in disappointment at the lack of attention she was getting. Then everything changed. The camera went behind her so all you could see was her back walking away but suddenly everyone was staring at her. Head after head turned to look after her as she walked by and the producers were well impressed. The camera then went to the front so that you could see Judy walking towards you. She was making a duck face and that was the reason everyone was turning to stare. I decided to try the same tactic.

I pushed my lips out to make a beak, blew my cheeks out, and made myself go cross-eyed. It worked a treat and Nose-picker nudged his mate who nudged his mate who nudged his mate and soon all the boys were staring at me with open mouths. I turned and skipped back to the girls.

"Result," I said as I punched the air.

"See," said Nesta. "I *told* you that you had the X factor. All the boys were looking. So now will you stop going on about being invisible and boys not noticing you? You got top score."

I couldn't keep it up anymore and showed them what I'd done. They all cracked up laughing and of course had to try it for themselves. As we made our way down the road, making the ugliest faces we could, everyone stared at us. It was hysterical. Of course that had to be the moment that we bumped into Mr. Johnson from school.

"Oh, for God's sake, girls," he said with a sigh as he went past. "When are you going to grow up?"

"Just testing to see if we have the X factor, sir," said Nesta.

"More like the Y factor," he said. "Why? Why? Why?"

When I got home later, my stepsister, Amelia was over visiting her dad. Angus was making tea in the kitchen and Amelia was curled up on the sofa watching TV so I went in to join her. We get on okay now but it took some time when Mum first married Angus and I found myself with two stepsisters, Amelia and Claudia, that I didn't particularly want. I was wary of them (I used to call them the wicked stepsisters) and I think that they were worried that I was going to usurp their position in their dad's heart but no chance of that—I really didn't like him for ages. I didn't give him a chance really; I even called him the lodger to help me deal with it. I thought he was boring and the girls were too good to be true, like a pair of little blonde Miss Perfects who had never done a thing wrong. Then one day Angus showed me photos of them in their punk phase. What a pair of maniacs. I almost felt sorry for Angus. We all get on great now. Almost like real family.

Amelia was watching a program about a group of women on a weight loss trial. Just my thing so I settled in with her.

"Why are you watching this?" I asked as Amelia has always been skinny.

"I love makeover programs," she replied as we gazed at the telly. "I love the before and afters. Like that woman there on the left of the screen with the short hair. She used to be massive and now look at her. Slimmed right down. She was saying that she was so unhappy before but no one realized as she used to play the joker so that everyone would like her and not realize how unhappy she was inside."

Sounds familiar, I thought. That's just what I was doing up in Muswell Hill doing my duck faces. Playing the fool, so that no one would realize how desperate I really feel inside.

"I want to lose weight," I said. "But it's soooo difficult. Especially hanging out with mates who are always eating and it doesn't help having a mum who insists on meals three times a day. And I have no will-power. It's as if I have no "stop" button when I smell or taste food. Before I can help myself, it's off the plate or out of the cupboard and in my mouth. If only someone could do my meals for me like for those women on the telly, then I wouldn't have to think about it."

"Best way is not to even think about diets," said Amelia. "You have to change the way you eat. Make healthy eating part of your life."

"I know, I *know*," I said with a sigh. "I've heard it all from Mum. The sensible approach blah de blah de blah . . . I've been cutting down this past week and it's felt like eternity. See, the thing is, I want to lose weight fast for a special occasion. I haven't got months to do it the sensible way."

"So what's the big occasion? I bet there's some boy you're trying to impress isn't there?"

"Yes and no," I said and told her a bit about Gabriel and all about *Teen Talk* and the fact that the TV puts ten pounds on you.

"Ah," said Amelia. "So you want a quick fix sort of thing?"

"Exactly."

"In that case, try what I did when I wanted to shift a few pounds for my wedding. Slim shakes."

"What are they?"

"Meal replacement drinks. You don't have to think about food at all, just have your slim shakes. They work a treat and they have all the stuff in them that you need to stay healthy."

Brilliant, I thought. Something new to try. I had ten pounds left from my Italian trip and Mum would give me next week's pocket money tomorrow. I could easily afford them, I decided. It was way too complicated trying to work out what was low fat, high fat, protein, carb and what size portion I could or couldn't have. Anyway, I didn't have weeks left before the pilot show to do it the sensible way. This sounded perfect for a quick result. Just have a shake three times a day and then there was nothing else to think about. I knew Mum would never agree to it but I got the details from Amelia and decided to buy some the next day.

At last I had the way forward. Exercise and slim shakes. I was going to be a skinny minnie in no time.

I'm in shape. Round is a shape.

# Chapter 11

# Doing the Camel

"We have so many different classes on offer," said the gym instructor when Mum went to sign us up the next day, "I suggest that you try a few of them and see what suits you best. It's important to enjoy what you do."

I couldn't wait. I'd try them all. I was fired up with enthusiasm, slim shakes hidden in my bag, and ready to do a different class every day after school to see which suited me best. Outside, the weather was still cold but the sun was shining for the first time in weeks. At last it was March, the winter months were behind us and spring was on its way. It felt symbolic of a new start. A new me.

Monday: I went for my first session in the gym. Karl, who is a total hunk (but not my type, too, er . . . bulgy in the lycra shorts department and legs like tree trunks), showed me how to use all the machines then stood there watching while I did my circuit. I was ready for a lie down after the first machine. It was called a cross trainer and, according to Karl, good for burning off calories. I thought I was going to die of a heart attack after about ten minutes. I carried on because Karl was watching and I didn't want to appear a total wimp, plus there were a couple of older guys there who had been going for ages and hadn't even broken into a sweat. After the cross trainer was the rowing machine. I gave it my all and pulled and pulled with all my might. By now, Karl was starting to annoy me as he said that if it had been a real boat, it would have sunk at the pace I was rowing. Very funny, not, I thought as I puffed and panted away.

Then there were machines for abs, machines for

triceps, biceps, machines for muscles I didn't even know I had.

By the end of forty-five minutes, I realized that all these machines aren't new at all. They were used in the Middle Ages to torture people in dungeons.

"No pain, no gain," Karl said, grinning, as I staggered out.

I decided the machines weren't for me. I'm more of the no pain, no pain school of philosophy and I had the rest of the week to find something I enjoyed and that didn't feel like punishment.

After my session, I went to treat myself to a little relaxation in the sauna. It was lovely and smelled fab because someone had put some eucalyptus oil on the burner. And then a bald old man came in and contributed his own aromatherapy. He did an SBD (silent but deadly). You've never seen a room clear so fast.

Slim shake report: two shakes, one vanilla for lunch, one chocolate for dinner. Not bad. Not great but they are drinkable. The trick, I realized, was to keep busy, busy, busy, and then I didn't think about my stomach growling.

Tuesday: Pilates class. I thought the Pilates class would be good after yesterday, as when I woke up this morning, every muscle in my body was aching. TJ recommended Pilates as she said it is gentle, stretches you out and is very effective. It sounded better than the pain of the machines so I decided to give it a try and was there bright and enthusiastic at four-thirty after school.

Ten minutes later, I was on a mat on the floor gasping with agony. Olga, the teacher was clearly a sadist, as she seemed to take great pleasure in see-ing others suffer.

"Breathe in, zip, breathe out," she'd cry as we lay on our backs with our legs suspended at ninety degrees, our heads up and our arms pumping at our sides. It was so complicated. You breathe in, you breathe out, you zip (which means pulling your tummy up and in as though zipping your jeans up only with Pilates you zip your flabby tummy in). I got totally confused as I didn't know when I was supposed to move, when to breathe in, when to zip, when to breathe out and I almost passed out through lack of oxygen. Still, it's early days, I told myself. Maybe I'll get the hang of it in the end.

Shake report: only managed one today at lunch because Mum was around at breakfast and supper. Strawberry. Didn't like it so only had half and my tummy did the rumble tum song again in afternoon classes. When people started giggling, I just called out, "It's sing along with Izzie's tum time, come along everyone, ah—one, two, three . . ."

I think some of the girls think I'm mad.

Wednesday: At school, TJ suggested I do a class at the gym that I really enjoyed, so I decided to go for one of the dance options. Salsa. Lucy came with me since you can pay to go to the dance classes without being a member of the gym. We both hoped that there would be loads of cute boys ready to groove on the dancefloor. Sadly, the only males at the class looked like they lived with their mothers which would have been okay if they were in their teens but they all looked about forty. My partner had two left feet and kept standing on my toes plus his shirt smelled like it hadn't been washed for days.

Shake report: a chocolate one at lunch-time and just for a change, hurrah, a slim a soup in the evening.

Discovered a side effect that wasn't mentioned on the packet. Wind. Stormy weather *à la* lower regions. Awful and I was in danger of being as bad as the man in the sauna on Monday doing SBDs all over the place. Eeeww.

Thursday: flamenco. Fab. This time Nesta came with me after school and we stomped our feet off. The teacher was a total babe with wild, dark, curly hair and black eyes like a gypsy and his class was full of women who were all clearly in love with him. Nesta took to it straight away but I found the footwork hard to do. Toe, heel, stomp, toe, heel, stomp. Stompity, stompity, stomp. Wave your arms gracefully in the air. It was going all right until I heel, toed then stomped on the foot of the lady who was dancing next to me. Then I almost whacked another lady's eye out with my arm movements. Maybe flamenco isn't my thing, I thought as the woman rubbed her eye then looked at me like she was going to produce a dagger from under her skirt and stab me with it.

Shake report: stormy weather *à la* tum is in danger of becoming a hurricane. Good God. Amelia didn't warn me about this. I spent all day with a strange expression on my face and couldn't concentrate much in classes. Partly because I was beginning to feel light-headed through lack of proper food and partly because I had to walk round with my buttocks clenched in case my lower half let rip and blew down one of the school walls. Not my best day.

Friday: Egyptian dance. *Yes!* At last I have found where I belong. Again, the class was all women but of all ages, shapes and sizes. And by shapes, I mean round, pear shape, apple. And by size, I mean from eight to eighteen. When the teacher said, "If you have a belly, all the better for the dance," I knew I had found my place. I loved the music and the time whizzed by as we wibbled, wobbled, and gyrated round the studio like a bunch of psychotic hippies. I didn't check my watch once to see how much longer we had to go and felt like I could have danced for hours.

Shake report: just one at lunch-time. Banana. Am beginning to think I could be a danger to the environment. This wind business is *no* joke. Lucy asked why I'd looked so worried all week and I was way too embarrassed to tell her. I decided to catch up on homework in the library at lunchtime, partly so that I didn't have to watch my mates eat but also to protect them from any windy pops I couldn't keep in.

On the way home from the Egyptian dance class I felt energized and enthusiastic. As there was no one around, I carried on practising the camel (a move from the class). You put your arm and a foot out in front of you, take a step forward as push your chest out, then curve back in as if pulling your tummy in, take a step back then step forward again while pushing forward with your belly so that your torso makes a sort of S-shape if seen from the side. It was hard to do gracefully so I was determined to get it right.

"Yo, move over Michael Jackson," said a voice behind me after I'd been going for a while.

I almost jumped out of my skin. "Who's that?" I said as I turned and came face to face with Josh, the local bad boy and one of my exes from last year.

"Where did you come from?"

"Ah. One of the great mysteries of the universe," he replied. "Where did I come from? Where am I going? Why am I here? Who knows?"

Same old Josh, I thought. He never could give a straight answer. He always had to be clever or evasive.

"So what were you doing?" he asked.

"Um, the camel," I said, then thought: if he can be evasive, so can I. "We're studying wildlife at school."

"Wildlife, huh? Well you can study me as part of your project any time."

I laughed. He was so flirty but I knew better than to respond. He was trouble with a capital T. My last encounter with him had led to me being out in the park in the middle of the night, throwing up all over him. A novel way to get a boy to remember you, Nesta had said at the time.

Still, it was good to see him and he accompanied me home and we chatted about what we'd been up to. I told him all about *Teen Talk* and being part of the audience.

"They're picking a panel," I told him, "but they'll probably pick all the skinny girls so that the show has babe appeal."

"Why should that give the show babe appeal?"

"You know, boys like thin girls."

"Says who?"

"Everyone knows that."

"No way. Most boys are just grateful if a girl likes them but most of all they want to hang out with someone who is fun. Course it helps if the girl is decent-looking like you . . ."

"Like me?"

"Yeah. You, but then you probably know that."

"Nah, I'm a frump."

Josh looked me up and down slowly and I felt myself begin to blush.

"You? A frump. No way. I've seen frump and you are the opposite end of the scale."

By the time we got to my house, I was beginning to feel a lot better about my shape. Josh felt it was his duty to give me a lecture on what boys found attractive and skinny didn't even come into it. When we reached my gate, I could tell he wanted to come in but I didn't want to risk it. I knew Josh. He'd want to smoke in my bedroom and probably had a bottle of vodka tucked in one of his pockets. He was one of the mad mistakes from my past that I didn't want to repeat.

> Philosophy of exercise
> Karl: No pain, no gain.
> Izzie: No pain . . . no pain.

# Chapter 12

# Clenched and Crimson

"Want to come to the gym, Angus?" I asked as I put on my coat on Saturday morning.

Angus grimaced and picked up the paper that was lying on the hall mat. "Er . . . think I'll give it a miss. Things to do."

"You should do something. Anything. Even if it's only walking."

"Hmph," he said. "Yes. Walking. I like long walks, preferably taken by people who annoy me, like you and your mother. Now off you go and leave me in peace."

I laughed. Angus could be quite funny when he wanted to be and I did feel for him. Mum had been as gung ho about trying the gym as I had and had been doing the classes after she'd finished work. Every supper time, she'd been nagging at Angus to go with her but he wasn't very enthusiastic preferring to stay at home with a gin and tonic and watch the history channel on cable.

It had worked out well for me though, because Mum was out every evening so she hadn't been able to keep her beady eye on what I had or hadn't been eating. I'd been able to stick to my slim shakes and bin what she'd cooked for supper. I'd lost three pounds and was feeling very virtuous and pleased with myself, if not a bit achy from all the classes and a tiny bit guilty about deceiving Mum. I'd been on the shakes for five days with only the occasional meal when Mum was around and I was definitely feeling thinner.

Our yoga instructor was a small wiry girl called Angie, and she started the class with a salute to the sun—a series of postures all put together in one fluid movement. I'd practiced it loads of times before at home as I have a book and a DVD show-ing how it's done but it felt good to be in a class and learn how to do it properly. However, as soon as I got to the part where you have to bend over, I felt my lower tummy rumble ominously. Oh hell, I thought as I squeezed my buttocks tight. Please no, please don't let me do an SBD and alienate myself from the group. Everybody would be bound to know that it was me. Luckily, as we carried on the feeling went and I began to relax and enjoy the class.

As the class progressed, we went into a shoulder stand, then Angie told us to roll further back and put our knees over our shoulders. Not the most elegant of positions as my stomach flopped for-ward over my trackie bottoms but everyone was in the same boat, so it didn't matter. But once again, came the feeling that a windy pop was on its way. Oh God, oh God, I thought as I clenched my but-tocks again, this is just horrendous. How can you relax and breathe when the lower part of your body is about to play a trumpet fanfare? I clenched even harder determined not to let it happen. Clearly I wasn't the only one as an elderly lady in the corner of the room, let one rip. She didn't seem fazed by it at all.

"Oops," she said, then laughed. "Sorry, everyone."

For a moment, I felt like I was going to get the giggles as I had an image of everyone having the same problem and that we were all lying there, pretending to be all serene and yoga-like when actually we were all clenching our buttocks for Britain.

As I lay there, clenched and crimson, I heard the studio door open, and footsteps.

"Sorry I'm so late," a male voice said to the teacher. "My bike got a puncture."

I strained to turn my neck so that I could see who had come in. Oh nooooo, I thought when I saw who it was and that he was laying out his mat behind me.

"Oh hi, Izzie." Gabriel grinned down at me. "We meet again."

"Umph . . . Gabriel! Hi." I smiled back, trying to act as if being red in the face, my bum in the air and knees over my shoulders was a perfectly normal position to be in when greeting someone. I lost my balance and fell over onto my side. "Oof."

Gabriel tried not to laugh as he knelt on his

mat, lay back, went smoothly into the position and somehow managed to look handsome even when upside down.

For the rest of the class, I couldn't concentrate. I was so aware of the angles that Gabriel was seeing me from as we went through the postures: the crab, the cat, the dog, the snake and so on. It was awful. In every position, my tummy was hanging out or he was face to face with my backside. Not a great way to make a good impression, I thought. He, on the other hand, seemed to have mastered all the positions and in each one, looked graceful and serene. Rats' droppings, I thought, I'd hoped I'd found a class that I wanted to do as well as the Egyptian dance but I'm not going to be able to come here every Saturday and look a fool in front of him.

When the class was over, I was about to scarper but he caught up with me and asked if I fancied a juice in the bar at the front of the gym. I agreed because I wanted his last impression of me to be the right way up, not on the floor doing the twisted snake or demented cat or whatever the positions were called.

"Been a member long?" he asked as we collected

our carrot and ginger drinks from the counter.

"Just joined," I said. "You?"

"Since last September," he said. "I come most Saturdays when there's nothing on in the TV studio."

Poo, I thought. That's yoga out then. It was one thing doing the lion (tongue out as far as you can stick it) when there were no boys around, another thing if the boy you fancied was right next to you. At least he didn't come to Egyptian dancing.

We chatted for about half an hour and, as before, got on really well. He was into all sorts of things that I am, like aromatherapy, crystals and astrology. He'd just moved out of his parents' house into lodgings and was really enthusiastic about doing up his room and living independently for the first time. It was nice to talk to a boy about stuff like that because all the ones I know aren't remotely interested in décor or paint colors.

"So what are you up to over the weekend?" he asked as we got up to go our separate ways.

"Oh, see my mates. Homework. Maybe do another class. You?"

"Working on my room." He reached into his

gym bag and produced a piece of paper on which he scribbled an address.

"Here. That's where I live now. If you've got a moment, pop over. You can tell me what you think of my color scheme. It's a bit of a mess still but almost ready for visitors."

Result, I thought. Maybe the sight of my bum hanging in the air when I did the snarling caterpillar didn't put him off after all.

"I'd love to," I said. "And I could bring my feng shui book if you're interested."

"Oh definitely," he said as we went out to the pavement from where he unchained a bike from a lamppost. "Okay then, see you around and come visit."

"Yeah." Definitely, I thought as he gave me a wave, got on his bike and rode away.

Halfway down the road, he stopped then circled back. I tried to look cool and pretended that I hadn't actually been staring at him on his bike. He stopped at the kerb next to me.

"And hey, if your mates have time, bring them too. The more the merrier. Now I have my own place I want it to be an open house. When I lived

at home with my parents, visitors were never welcome. My dad is an unsociable old codger. I really,
really want my new place to be different, with
people dropping in all the time."

And off he rode again. I felt confused. Bring my
mates? Why? Wouldn't he want to be alone with
me? Did he fancy me or not? What was going on?

After the gym, I went over to TJ's to meet the girls.
TJ's house was only a short walk from the gym but
by the time I got there, I felt exhausted and faint
with hunger having only had a vanilla shake and
carrot juice so far that day. Lucy, TJ, and Nesta
were in the kitchen with croissants and hot chocolates, talking about going to the mall or Camden
as TJ wanted a break because she'd been in all
morning working on the school magazine.

"And Lucy needs cheering up," said Nesta.

"Why? What's happened?" I asked.

"Nothing," she said. "I'm fine."

"Tony's got his interview for Oxford," said
Nesta. "The letter came this morning. If they make
him an offer, he'd be mad not to go."

"I know that," said Lucy. "I've been ready for it

all along. That's why I've been trying to cool it with him. Well, that and the wandering hands . . ."

"Has he started with that again?" asked Nesta.

Lucy shook her head. "No. He's been very well behaved but you know it was the reason we broke up before Italy."

"Oh let's go out and meet loads of new boys," said Nesta. "Distractions. New love interests."

"Yeah," said TJ. "First one to get a date with a new boy wins."

Although it sounded like a fun afternoon was planned, I had no energy. I wanted to crawl up to the nearest bedroom, lie on a bed and go to sleep.

"You guys go," I said. "I'll just go home and vegetate, that is if I can get there. I can hardly walk after all the classes I've done this week."

"You've been overdoing it," said TJ. "Three classes a week is enough to be fit. How many have you done?"

"One every day but only because I wanted to find out which ones I want to do," I said, then went on to fill them in on seeing Gabriel again at yoga.

"He's probably just playing it cool," said Lucy.

"Wants to get to know you better before he makes his move."

"Maybe," I said. "But maybe the sight of my bum in the air put him off."

Nesta made a disapproving face. "Oh, for heaven's sake, Izzie, you've got a great bum. All you seem to go on about these days is how awful you look or what diet you're on. And at school, you hide in the library and then take off afterwards to the gym. We've hardly seen you this week."

"We hung out at the flamenco class," I objected, "and Lucy, you came with me to salsa."

"Not the same," said Lucy. "We used to spend time having a laugh in the lunch break then after school. It's like you've got so serious about all this losing weight lark. Where's the old fun Izzie?"

"Here," I said. "Just a bit knackerooed at the moment. And I am still fun. Remember last weekend? Discovering the X factor. That was fun."

"I agree with TJ," said Nesta. "I think you're overdoing the classes. You need to chill out a bit, spend proper time with mates and eat something besides those stupid shakes."

I looked at them sitting there. A familiar scene

with mugs of steaming chocolate, croissants in hands, jam pots open, crumbs all over the table. It wasn't fair that I had to deny myself once again when they could eat and enjoy it. Food was such a bonding thing at all times of the year: cakes on birthdays, pizza and a DVD on rainy nights, toast and peanut butter when you're starving and back from school, mince pies at Christmas, Sunday lunches for catching up with family, muffins at the mall with mates. I was beginning to feel left out and even though it was only two weeks since I'd been trying to lose weight, it felt like I'd been denying myself forever.

TJ's mum, Dr. Watts, came in from the utility room where she'd been putting the washing on.

"What's all this about classes?" she asked. "And shakes?"

"Izzie," said TJ. "She's joined the gym to lose weight."

"Ah," said Dr. Watts. "Cardiovascular exercise. That's what's best for losing weight. Anything that gets the heart pumping."

"Just the sight of the cute instructors there does that for me," said Nesta. "Does that count?"

Dr. Watts laughed. "Not exactly. But what's all this about you wanting to lose weight, Izzie?"

Here we go, I thought. Mention that you want to lose weight to an adult and they all feel the need to give a lecture.

Dr. Watts sat down at the table and looked at me with concern. "Does your mum know that you're trying to lose weight?"

"Yeah. Course."

"And how are you going about it?" she asked. "What's this about shakes?"

I felt like I was a criminal being cross-examined. "Er . . ."

"First she spent a week starving herself," Lucy burst out. "And now she's drinking only slim shakes and her stomach rumbles like mad in school and . . . well, we're worried about her."

Oh thanks a lot, I thought. Why not tell her all my secrets while you're at it?

Dr. Watts's concerned look grew. "Oh, Izzie," she said. "That's not the way to go about it. On those diets, yes, some weight appears to come off quickly but a lot of it is water and the moment you start eating properly again, it all piles on again. If you deprive your body of proper food, it goes onto alert, thinking that you're starving and then burns what food you are eating slowly to compensate. Then the moment you start eating properly again, the weight goes straight back on because your system is still trying to protect you by burning up food slowly. And as for those slim shakes, you may as well eat a good nutritious meal as it would probably contain the same calories. The only way to lose weight and keep it off is to do it slowly, aim for a loss of a pound or two a week."

"That's what Mum said," I groaned, "but that will take forever."

"Well, the weight doesn't go on overnight and it's not going to come off overnight, no matter what mad fad diet you do."

Yeah, yeah, I thought, I've heard it all before.

"A good eating plan and exercise, that's the way to do it for a permanent weight loss," continued Dr. Watts.

"But it's *so* hard . . ."

"It needn't be," said Dr. Watts. "I always advise the people who come to me wanting to lose weight to join a club. That way, you learn about healthy eating and you have the support of a group. If you're really serious about it and your mum agrees, I could give you a note—under-sixteens need one to join a slimming club in this country."

She got up, rooted around in a drawer and pulled out a leaflet. "Here you are. Weight Winners. There's a class on Monday evening and it's not far from you, just at the top of East Finchley High Road."

I pulled a face. I felt tired. Tired of the shakes. Tired of feeling tired. Tired of the windy pops. Tired of feeling left out of the good time munchie moments.

"Really," continued Dr. Watts, "you don't have to starve to lose weight. It's just a question of eating the right foods and the weight will come right off in no time. And with the right plan, you can even have a little treat every now and again."

I nodded. I was beginning to realize that she was right. Maybe I should try a more sensible approach. There was no way I could do another week on the slim shakes. I felt weird and light-headed and the idea of a decent meal was very tempting. "Okay," I said. "I'll give it a go."

"Hurrah!" said Lucy. "Because we want Izzie back, no matter what shape or size she is."

Later that night, I sat down to a plate of pasta with Mum and Angus and enjoyed every minute of it. Mum was all for me joining the club when she heard that Dr. Watts had given it the okay.

"As long as you do it sensibly," she said as she watched me bolt down my food. "You have to have balance."

I picked up two cookies from the plate on the table and held one each hand.

"There you go. A balanced diet. A cookie in either hand."

Angus laughed but Mum pursed her lips. "Honestly, Izzie. I despair sometimes. It's always all or nothing with you. One minute you're eating hardly anything, the next, you eat everything that's in front of you. Why can't you find a happy medium?"

"I will. I will, at the club. Dr. Watts said they teach a healthy eating plan there."

"Well, I hope so," said Mum. "You've been looking peaky this week and I've been worried about you."

"No need," I said. "Mad fad diets are not for me, believe me."

After supper, I felt so much better just for having eaten. And I had a day and a half before I joined the club. A day and a half to eat all the things I would never be able to eat again, ever, for all eternity. Better make the most of it, I thought as I snuck into the kitchen later to find Mum's treat tin.

"Izzie, what are you doing?" she asked when she caught me with a fudge bar in my hand.

"New diet," I said with a weak grin. "I've tried the Atkins diet, this is the Fatkins diet."

Mum looked up to heaven. "You're mad."

"No, I'm not." I grinned back at her. "I'll start properly on Monday. Promise."

"Yeah, yeah. Heard that one before," said Mum as she went back in to watch telly.

A balanced diet: a cookie in each hand.

# Starstruck

"Arghhhhhhhhhhhhhhhhhhhhhh!"

I wanted to kick something. Or someone. It was Monday morning and I'd just weighed myself. My weight was exactly the same as last Monday. *Exactly*. Urghhhhhhhhh. I felt soooo frustrated. After all that I'd been through! The wind, the stomach gurgles, the feeling like I was going to pass out. And for what? For *this*! I wanted to chuck the scales right out of the window. Dr. Watts was blooming right about slim shakes. You lose some weight. Yahey. You eat again and it all goes straight back on. Bummer. Still, I guess the "last ever in the world for all eternity" cookies on Saturday evening, slice of pizza at

Ben's during band practice on Sunday, portion of chips on the way back from my guitar lesson with Lucy's dad and the final final *final* bowl of ice cream last night after I'd dropped round to Gabriel's with Lucy (he wasn't in) hadn't exactly helped. But it was no more than the others had. They just never seemed to gain an ounce. Pfff.

Breathe, I told myself, calm down. It's okay. There is hope.

New week. New start. I was going to join the Weight Winner's club tonight and learn how to drop a few pounds sensibly. I was well ready for it. I'd had enough of my own mad roller-coaster ways of doing it.

After school, I went and had a swim at the gym, then made my way up the high street to find the hall where the meeting was being held.

Oh no, I thought when I got close and finished off my "last ever in the whole of eternity and beyond and even after that" fudge bar. A load of boys I knew were sitting on a wall opposite the hall. Biff from the band was there, plus a few of his mates from Lal's school. They were laughing and smoking fags and messing about. No way could I go past them and into the slimming club. It would be all around North London in no time.

I felt so disappointed. I'd been pinning my hopes on this. I quickly called Nesta on my mobile and explained my dilemma.

"I'll be right there," she said. "Meet you down by the pharmacy in ten minutes and I'll distract them for you while you sneak in. I've been doing my history homework and am bored out of my mind so I need something to do."

I hovered round a corner waiting for her and by the time she appeared, the boys had pushed off, no doubt to sit on another wall somewhere. Such is the glamorous life of teenage boys in Finchley.

"Sorry, false alarm," I said as Nesta looked around for the boys.

"Never mind," said Nesta. "I'll come to the class with you."

"You?"

"Yeah. It will be good experience in case I ever have to play someone with weight problems when I'm an actress."

"Hardly, Nesta. I mean who would cast you as a fatty?"

Nesta rolled her eyes. "Haven't you ever heard of padding? Costumes? Come on, let's go in."

I didn't object as I'd been feeling nervous about going in on my own so it was nice to have some company.

Inside the hall were an assortment of women, some young, some old, some slim, some really enormous. One large lady gave Nesta a strange look as if to say, why are you here?

Nesta beamed at her and did a twirl. "I've lost four stone so far. This plan really works if you stick to it."

She sat down next to the lady, who was called Jean, and soon they were like old pals, swapping tips and recipes. You have a great career as a character actress ahead of you Nesta Williams, I thought as I went to register.

Our group leader was a middle-aged blonde lady called Shirley and as the meeting got going, I settled in to listen to what she had to say.

"No mad lose-a-stone-in-a-week diets here," she said, "because they don't work. . . ."

As she went on to explain the plan, it sounded

reasonable enough. All foods were listed in a booklet and each one was given a number of stars, for example: an apple, half a star; a chunk of cheddar cheese, six stars! A piece of bread, one and a half stars. A pizza, five million thousand stars. A tub of my favorite ice cream, ten thousand trillion stars. Well, a lot of stars, anyway. It was beginning to dawn on me why my weight had been fluctuating. In Florence, I must have been swallowing a whole blooming solar system every day.

"Each day you're allowed between eighteen and twenty stars depending on your start weight plus as many vegetables as you like," continued Shirley.

"Puts a whole new meaning on being starstruck," whispered Nesta.

"I know, I've been a celestial disaster so far," I whispered back.

However, it sounded simple enough and what I liked was the fact that no food was excluded, it was just a question of totting up the stars and not eating too many that were star loaded.

I turned to the part of the booklet that listed chocolate. Two squares of any type = one and a half stars. Four squares = three stars. Eight squares

= six stars. In most bars, there are about twelve squares so I quickly did my maths. A bar would be about nine stars. Two bars a day, eighteen stars, and I'd have used up my allowance.

"So are you saying that if I wanted to use up my stars on chocolate that I could?" I asked.

"Or on wine?" asked Jean.

Shirley smiled. "You could, in theory, but that wouldn't leave you many stars left for proper food, and you'd end up feeling depleted. Sugar is like empty food, no nutritious value. No. This plan is about learning to eat the right foods. Read the booklets and try and pick a range of foods from all the food groups: protein, carbohydrate, a little fat, lots of fresh fruit and vegetables and then you can have a little chocolate or wine as long as you allow for it in your star allowance."

Cool, I thought. I could do this. And fruit was low in stars, vegetables were star free so I'd be able to eat plenty.

"Make sure you keep a food diary in the first week," advised Shirley, "so that I can see if you've got the hang of it. And *don't* weigh yourself every day. Weight fluctuates up and down in a week and a daily weigh-in won't give you an accurate reading."

Tell me about it, I thought.

After running through the rules, Shirley got round to the task of weighing the members in. It was hilarious. If someone lost a pound or so, she rang a bell and everyone clapped. If someone hadn't lost any weight or had put on some, she'd frown and wag her finger at them and tell them to try harder next week and they'd slink away, then have a giggle at the back of the class.

It was going to be okay, I thought. They were a nice bunch of women and it wasn't embarrassing at all.


After the class, Nesta and I did a detour to the house where Gabriel lived. It was on North Road between East Finchley and Highgate and was a huge, old Victorian place set back from the road. Judging by the number of bells in the porch, it looked like about twelve people lived there.

"Who's there?" Gabriel's voice came through the intercom after I'd rung the bell with his name on.

"Um . . . Izzie and Nesta," I said.

He buzzed us in and we entered a brown and

dingy hallway. It had paint peeling off the walls and smelled like old welly boots and boiled cabbage. We stepped over a pile of junk mail on the floor, squeezed our way past a pile of bikes, and then Gabriel appeared at the top of the stairs.

"I'm up here," he said, beaming at us. "Come on in."

"We were just passing," I replied as we made our way up.

"I'm so pleased you dropped by," said Gabriel as he ushered us along the corridor. So am I, I thought. Poor Gabriel having to live in a dump like this, he probably needs some company to cheer him up.

He opened his door with a flourish. "Sorry about the mess. I haven't finished yet."

Once inside his room, another world opened up. It was like stepping into something off one of the makeover shows on telly. The place was immaculate with soft gold lighting from a couple of elegant lampshades. In the centre of the room was a huge double bed with a dark red cover folded neatly back and behind it a Japanese black lacquered screen. One wall he'd painted red like the bedcover, the others he'd done a pale cream.

The whole effect looked simple and stylish.

"Wow," said Nesta as she looked at a gold Thai statue of a goddess in the fireplace. "I've seen these at Camden Lock. Looks great."

Gabriel looked pleased by her reaction. "Yeah. I got it from a stall there. So what do you think, Izzie?"

"Fab and a half," I said as I gazed at some Japanese prints he had framed on one wall. "But it's one room. Do you have a kitchen or bathroom tucked away somewhere?"

Gabriel grimaced. "Ah. That's the down side of student accommodation. I have to share the kitchen and bathroom with a bunch of yobs. Um . . . I think I'll spare you that experience for now as some of them don't know the meaning of cleaning up. No. This is my oasis."

"You've done a great job," I said. "I can't think what you meant by saying the place was still a mess. It looks perfect to me."

"Still got a way to go," said Gabriel as he pointed to few unopened boxes next to a futon with cushions at the far end of the room. "Take a seat. I was about to make some coffee. Want some? Or juice?"

"Coffee, please," we chorused.

"Kenyan or Columbian?"

"Oh . . . er . . . Nesta, what do we like?" I asked.

"Strong and sassy like our men," said Nesta as she flopped down on the futon.

"You choose," I said.

Gabriel laughed. "Won't be a moment. Make yourself at home."

Before he left, he quickly lit a candle and the aroma of jasmine began to fill the air. "Just in case anyone's cooking something disgusting," he said. "Don't want it coming through."

"That smells divine," said Nesta.

"Yeah. I like nice smells, as Izzie already knows. Tuberose, Jo Malone, right?"

"Right," I said. He'd remembered. That must mean something.

While Gabriel was out making coffee, Nesta knelt on the floor and looked at his bookshelf. "You can tell a lot about a person by what's on his shelves," she said.

I went to kneel next to her. There was a complete mixture. Books on interior design. Books on film and media studies. Loads of videos of old black and white movies. A copy of *The Wizard of*

*Oz*. Couple of novels by people I didn't know. Photo albums. I was really tempted to have a peek but didn't dare in case he came back in.

"This guy has taste," said Nesta as she sat back on the futon and looked around with approval.

Gabriel came back in with fresh coffee (he grinds his own beans!) and filled us in on some of the other people that lived in the house. Marcus, menopausal at twenty-three; David, love god (Nesta took note of his name for future reference); Oliver the computer geek who never went out and only ate Pot Noodles; Jon the shy boy down from the Midlands who was over-awed by college life and a bit lonely; Jamie the hypochondriac; Eric the prankster . . .

"It sounds like half the student body of London live here," said Nesta.

"Any girls?" I asked, trying to sound casual.

"Mary and Nicola on the top floor. They share. They're okay. At least they're clean."

"You should write it all down," I said when we'd stopped laughing over a story he told us about a time when Eric put chili powder in Jamie's hemorrhoid cream. "All these characters, it would make a great book."

He pointed to a computer on a desk. "Already started," he said, grinning. "I'm about halfway through."

He was great company, full of enthusiasm for the media course he was on and what he wanted to do when he'd finished. And he was so interested in Nesta and me and what we wanted to do when we left school. Nesta told him all about wanting to be an actress and I told him about being in the band King Noz and wanting to be a singer-songwriter. He tried to get me to sing something but I told him I couldn't without my guitar. I liked him more and more. He didn't only look good but he was interesting and interested in others. Some boys I've known only ever talk about themselves and didn't even bother to find out what made me tick, whereas he seemed genuinely fascinated.

"So what do you think?" I asked when Nesta and I left. "Do you think he likes me?"

"Oh yeah," she said. "He clearly likes you a lot."

"So worth pursuing?"

Nesta hesitated. "Yes. But . . ."

"But what?"

"It's like he's . . . I don't know. There's something

going on with him that I can't put my finger on."

"What?"

"Not sure . . ."

This was frustrating. Nesta was the expert on reading boys. She can usually spot a dud or a problem a mile off.

"Oh come on, Nesta . . ."

"It's nothing bad. The opposite, in fact; it's like he's too good to be true. He's like the perfect guy."

"I thought the perfect guy was one who snogged you, then turned into a pizza," I said, quoting the old joke.

"Pizza? Not for you anymore, my dear," said Nesta. "Too many stars. Your perfect guy now would be one who snogged you then turned into a bowl of organic salad. *Deux* stars."

I laughed. "I know what you mean about Gabriel, though. He is close to perfect but I don't see why that should worry you. I knew there had to be a perfect boy out there somewhere and here he is alive and well and living around the corner." I really hoped he asked me out when we saw him again on Saturday.

★ ★ ★

The next day, I began my food diary.

Tuesday: excellent. Eighteen stars. Cereal for brekkie, low-fat sandwich at lunch, lots of fruit and vegetables, medium baked potato in the evening. Feel great. Almost normal and not so obsessed with food.

Wednesday: twenty stars, two on a bit of choc at Lucy's.

Thursday: almost got blown round at Ben's at band practice as he ordered pizza again. Pizzas are mega stars and if I'd had a piece, it would have taken me over my star ration, but it seems to be the only food that Ben knows of. Had a tiny bit so felt like I didn't miss out and counted it into my allowance. At home later, Mum had got a cake as it was Angus's birthday. I felt it would be churlish not to have any so I counted up how many stars I had left. One. So had an itsy-bitsy, tiny piece. Could have been a celestial disaster with too many stars but no, I kept it together. Feel so much better on this plan as I can eat normally. Just maybe less than I did before, like instead of having two bits of chocolate cake, I'll just have a small slice.

Friday: I am definitely feeling thinner and had a

sneak weigh in to discover that I had lost two and a half pounds! Excellent. And amazing as I feel like I am eating normally, only difference is that instead of piling my plate with roast spuds, I pile it with other veg.

After doing my homework on Friday, I sat down to watch telly while I totted up my daily stars. There was a program on about a country in Africa that had been suffering from a drought. As I sat there, I began to feel more and more guilty about how I'd been behaving over the last few weeks. I'd thought about food nonstop, what I could and couldn't eat, how I looked. Me, me, me. I'd even binned food that Mum had cooked for me, and there on the same planet as me were thousands of people with nothing to eat at all. They didn't have the luxury of wondering how they looked in clothes as they hardly had anything to wear except rags and other people's cast-offs. I felt awful. *Really* awful and I felt my eyes fill up with tears. I am the worst person in the world, bad and selfish, I thought as I watched a mother who looked like a skeleton try to feed a baby with a tummy swollen from lack of food.

Mum came in and caught me wiping my eyes.

"Izzie, what is it?"

I pointed at the television. "All those people. They don't have enough to eat and I . . . I . . ."

"You what, love?"

"I'm such a *bad* person. All I've done for the past few weeks is moan and groan and feel sorry for myself and all the time there are people starving. It all feels so wrong."

Mum smiled sadly. "Isn't it supposed to be me who's saying that to you? The classic parent speech, you must eat your supper, think about all the hungry people in the world . . ."

"I think you did when I was younger. It never really registered before now though."

Mum sat on the edge of the sofa. "I know what you mean." She sighed. "There's such an imbalance. It doesn't seem right, does it? Sometimes when I'm at the supermarket, I watch myself and everyone else pile everything into our trolleys, especially, say, at Christmas when we all go mad and buy more than we need. We're so lucky that we have everything when others have no home or food."

"I *hate* myself," I said as more images of hungry families flashed across the screen. "I've been so selfish."

"Oh Izzie, you mustn't beat yourself up just because you were trying to lose a bit of weight. I know there are so many things that aren't right in the world but you're a fifteen-year-old girl and living in our society, you have different pressures on you. It's perfectly natural that you want to look your best."

Duh, I thought. This is a turn around from her earlier objections to me cutting down on food.

"I wish I could do something though. What can I do?" I asked.

"You've made a start, Izzie," said Mum. "You've noticed. You care. Some people don't even give others a second thought."

"I *hate* to think that people are suffering while we have it all and yet most of the time, I don't think about it for a second."

"Yes, but suffering is relative you know. You have to remember that. It's not only people in those countries that suffer. So do people who appear to have it all. I know that yes, some people suffer for physical reasons, like having no food or clothing. But so do families over here. Different pressures, different stresses. Loneliness, loss, poverty, bad health, it happens over here too."

I was beginning to feel really depressed. And helpless. "But what can *I* do?"

"Oh lots, Iz, and I'm sure you will, knowing you. Start by being aware of when people are suffering for whatever the reason. Here *and* there. There's no guarantee for happiness because we live in a more affluent society; and no certainty of an easy ride for anyone, however fortunate they are or which culture they live in. Rich people who seem to have it all still experience loss, disappointment, illness, death of loved ones. Life can be a roller coaster for all of us. You have to reach out and grab the good times."

I looked at Mum in amazement. I'd never heard her talk like that before. She was usually too busy rushing around with her job or telling me what to do. I'd never thought of her as some-one who was aware of people in need.

"I guess," I said. "I often look at people and wonder, are you happy? What's your life like? What's your story?"

"That's a good start. Be aware. Small steps in the

beginning because you are only fifteen with your whole life in front of you to do what you can. And I know it makes you sad to see this on TV but I'm glad it affects you. It means you have a heart and I'm sure in time, you'll do something about it."

I nodded. And I would think about what I could do, then act on it. I'd become more aware as sometimes I don't like to watch programs like the one that was on because it makes me feel so rotten but I guess that sticking my head in the sand and pretending it wasn't happening wasn't going to help much. Sometimes I hated watching the news as there seems to be so much that is wrong in the world. So many innocent people dying in wars that aren't of their making or being hungry when all that we need is here on the planet if we could redress the imbalance. It was all upside down. Why oh why can't we all live together and share our resources, I wondered and does it really matter if my bum is slightly too big when there are people on the planet who are starving?

"It's a mad, mad world," I said.

Mum nodded. "Isn't it? But it's also a fab, fab world. Some people make donations, others do charity events to raise money, others give their time, others their talent, others who are in a position to do so can give their name to a project and suddenly everyone wants to be a part of it just because a celebrity has become involved. Just don't be one of the people who turn their head and say not my problem."

"I won't," I said. "I won't turn my head."

---

### Every Drop Counts
#### written by Izzie

Last night a hand reached out to me
Its arm withered by want and apathy
Another drought in a nameless place
Another hungry child with flies on its face
I close my eyes and avoid the news
I've seen it all before, the children always lose

Tiny fingers, tiny hands
Broken hearts in a stranger's land

Whatever I do, whatever I say,
It won't make the world spin a different way
Whatever I think, whatever I dream

Won't make this image appear less obscene
Won't do no good to sing, cry and shout
My floods of tears won't end the drought

Tiny fingers, tiny hands
Broken hearts in a stranger's land

Think again, think again
I'm too wrapped up in my pain
Gotta wake up and walk into reality
Any self doubt is just a triviality
And though my voice sounds pretty small
If we shout together, we can break down walls

Tiny fingers, tiny hands
Broken hearts in a stranger's land

Whatever we do, whatever we say
We can still make a difference, starting today
With a drop at a time, if we work as a team
We can all take a bucket down to the stream
Soon a river of compassion, a flood of joy

# Chapter 14

# Pilot
## Show

"I wonder what's going on," said Nesta, after we'd signed in and made our way into the studio on Saturday morning. John was running around the aisles looking as though he was going to have a heart attack. Geena was heatedly talking into a mobile phone and there was an air of panic in the place.

I on the other hand was feeling calm and more confident that I had in ages. I was wearing the pin-striped Cyberdog top with my jeans and both Lucy and TJ had told me how good I looked. Ready to be noticed this time, I thought as I spotted Gabriel at the back of the hall, and then went over to him.

"What's happening?" I asked.

"Oh, the usual disasters on a live show. Sue from the panel hasn't shown up. And our guest singer is stuck on a train somewhere north of Birmingham. Doubt if he's even going to make it."

"Izzie can sing," Lucy piped up behind me.

"No way. Shut up," I said. "And anyway, they don't want just anyone on. They want a celebrity guest."

Gabriel studied my face. "You up for it, Iz? I remember you telling me about your songs."

"She's brilliant," said Nesta. "She could easily do it."

"They won't want me," I insisted. Although I'd felt ready to be noticed by Gabriel, being noticed by thousands of viewers was another matter altogether and the thought of it made me quake inside.

"Well, quite honestly, anybody would save the day at the moment," said Gabriel before calling John over. "Hey, John, over here. Potential guest replacement. Izzie. Singer-songwriter."

I gave Lucy a filthy look and she gave me one

back *and* stuck her tongue out at me. She pulled me aside and whispered, "This is your chance. Show the world who you are, you idiot."

John looked me up and down doubtfully. "Can you really sing?"

"Yeah but . . . no, but . . . yeah, I can. I do."

"Have you ever sung in public?"

"Loads of times," said Nesta. "She's in a band called King Noz. She writes her own songs too."

I gave Nesta a swift kick.

"Ow," she said, then rubbed her shin.

"What do you play?" asked John. "Piano or guitar?"

"Oh . . . guitar but . . ."

"Come with me."

I gave Nesta an "I'll get you later" look and followed him to the back of the studio, down a corridor and into a dressing room.

"Give me five minutes," said John and disappeared.

I took a look around. This must be how it is when you really are a celebrity guest I thought as I took in the white washed room, enormous bunch of flowers, Evian water and bowl of fruit arranged on a low coffee table.

John was back before I knew it with a guitar in hand and Gabriel not far behind him.

"Okay, play," said John.

I took the guitar and plucked a few notes. "Give me a moment."

"Haven't got a moment," he said, turning to Gabriel. "Right, we're okay for the second spot, we'll go out on the prerecording of Alicia." Then he turned back to me. "Ready?"

I took a deep breath. Ready as I will ever be, I thought, and sang some of the song I'd written last night after talking to Mum about people starving in some parts of the world.

I didn't look up at John or Gabriel as I sang. I just tried to focus on getting the words right. ". . . *Tiny fingers, tiny hands, broken hearts in a stranger's land . . .*"

When I'd finished, I glanced up.

Gabriel gave me the thumbs-up and grinned. John's expression still looked harassed. He looked at what I was wearing.

"Hhm," he said as he looked at my top. "Nice out-fit but those stripes won't work. Get her into makeup, Gabriel, and see what there is in costumes."

And with that, he ran out.

"What did he mean?" I asked.

Gabriel beamed at me. "You're on."

"Oh. Wow. So why can't I wear this top?"

"Vertical lines distort like mad on camera," said Gabriel. "Come on. We'll find you something else. Let's get going."

For the next half hour, I barely had time to think. Gabriel rushed me into makeup and stood and advised the makeup girl as she brushed various powders onto my face.

"Not too heavy on the eyes, keep it light but maybe a little shadow round the corners. Excellent," said Gabriel. "Lots of lip-gloss."

My hair was blown even straighter than it normally is; then it was out of there, down another corridor and into a costume department where Gabriel went into hyperdrive.

"Right," he said as he flicked through rail after rail and scoured shelf after shelf. "I know exactly what I'm looking for. Shoe size?"

"Thirty-eight," I said.

After a few moments, he chucked a pair of fab brown-leather cowboy boots at me. "Get these on," he said as he looked me up and down. "Size?"

"Um . . . fourteen, maybe . . ."

"Never. Twelve. We'll keep the jeans you're in but I want . . ." He started flicking through the rails again. "Ah, how about this?"

He'd picked out the most exquisite camisole. It was vintage in style, lilac crêpe silk with a tiny bit of lace around the dipped neckline and a ribbon crisscross over the boobs. "Try it on."

I wasn't about to strip off in front of him, especially as I had one of my faded white bras on. "Turn round," I said.

"Oh right, yes, course, sorry." Gabriel turned.

I quickly stripped my black top off and slipped into the camisole.

"Done?" asked Gabriel.

"Yes but . . ."

Gabriel turned, gave me the once over then he let out a slow whistle. "Perfect," he said. "That'll get them going. Perfect, perfect."

"Can I look?"

He took my hand and pulled me back down the corridors and back into the dressing room where he stopped in front of the mirror.

I took a look.

"Ohmigod. It's too tight. My boobs! I look . . ."

"Izzie, you look great," said Gabriel. "Absolutely *great*. It's not tight at all. It fits like a glove. You should wear more stuff like this."

I didn't have time to object any further as John stuck his head round the door. "Ready? Hey, Izzie, you look lovely."

Gabriel nodded. "Doesn't she?"

"We've just started on the first discussion then we'll go to Izzie. Get her in place."

I grabbed the guitar and we were out of the dressing room, along another maze of corridors and led to the side of the stage where the audience discussion was going great guns.

I could hardly breathe, it was all happening so fast.

"Are you going to do the song you did in the dressing room?"

"Er, yes . . . sure. If that's okay."

"Whatever you're comfortable with," said Gabriel, then his bleeper bleeped. He checked his message. "Okay, wait for Geena to introduce you then off you go. And, Izzie, remember to smile. And stand up straight. I know this may feel nerve-wracking but act confident. No one will ever know you're shaking inside."

"Right. Smile, stand up straight," I replied. "Confident. Oh God." And breathe, I told myself.

I heard Geena rounding up the discussion and then go into my intro: ". . . and now, at great expense, all the way from North London, we have our very own . . . Izzie Foster."

Gabriel pushed me forward and I walked on to the stage and into what seemed like blinding lights. It took me a moment to adjust my eyes and see the microphone. Oh God, my knees have turned to jelly, I thought as I walked forward. Oh please, don't let me freeze. Let me get this next few minutes over with. Confident, confident. I took another deep breath, went up to the microphone and beamed a big smile.

"Hello, Camden," I called out into the studio.

"Hello, Izzie," the audience called back.

It was a dream come true. A moment I'd fantasized about so many times in front of the mirror at home. Just relax, I told myself. Imagine that you're at one of the gigs with Ben and King Noz. It's just another number.

"I'm going to sing you a song I wrote only last night," I said, "and I hope that some of you might agree with the way I feel."

Then I went into the song. As I was singing, I tried to really feel the words. And I did feel the words as time seemed to stand still.

". . . *Tiny fingers, tiny hands, broken hearts in a stranger's land . . .*"

When I'd finished, the place erupted. I'd done it. It was okay. I'd remembered all the lines and people were clapping, some even stomping their feet. I caught sight of Lucy and Nesta in the audience. They were jumping up and down and going ballistic.

"Cue to break," I heard John say somewhere in the studio. I felt stunned and next thing I knew, Gabriel and Nesta were hugging me.

"Izzie, you were totally brilliant, just *brilliant*," Nesta gushed.

"A star is born," said Gabriel with a big smile. "You saved the day."

John came over and patted me on the back. "Nice one, Izzie. Well done."

I scanned the audience for Lucy but couldn't see

her but a moment later, she was hugging me too.

"God, Izzie, I felt so proud," she said and I swear she had tears in her eyes. "I couldn't believe it was really you up there. You looked so confident. 'Hello, Camden.' Like, wow . . . You sounded like such a pro."

I laughed. I felt brilliant. Performing in front of a live audience is the best high in the world, I thought as we made our way off the stage and back into the audience for the second half.

"And you look so good," said Lucy. "I couldn't have picked a better outfit for you myself."

I hugged her back. Life was good and with the way that Gabriel had been paying me so much attention, I had a feeling that it was about to get even better.

# Hot or Not?

The second half of the show got off to a great start and everyone seemed to have loads to say. Gabriel told me that the phone lines had been going bonkers after my song, and people had been ringing in from all over the country to say they wanted to hear more from me. I thought my five minutes of fame was over and I was going to be able to relax in the audience and enjoy the rest of the show while I caught my breath. But no, John told me to join the panel and that they were going to pick up on a new theme for the second discussion.

When I heard what the topic was going to be, I thought it couldn't have been more relevant, as least to me anyway. The topic was: hot or not? And I soon found out that I wasn't the only one who worried about whether I was or not. It was clearly a subject close to everyone's heart—feeling inadequate or invisible to the opposite sex. Boys and girls both joined in with gusto and it was fascinating to hear the boys say, time and time again, that they didn't want a picture perfect girlfriend. They didn't want the teen queen from the magazine, they wanted normal. Fun. Confident. And curvy.

After the show, Gabriel was kept busy, clearing the stage and helping the camera crew. Lucy, Nesta and I sat at the back for a while, reliving it all; everyone seemed to be hanging about, reluctant to leave. Finally, the studio started emptying and we got up to go. I looked for Gabriel, but couldn't see him.

"Just a moment," I said to Lucy and Nesta. "I want to find Gabriel and say thanks." And give him a chance to ask me out, I thought as I made my way down to the stage area to find him. I was feeling on top of the world and more confident that I had in ages. I was on a roll. How could he resist?

He didn't appear to be anywhere.

"Seen Gabriel?" I asked a cameraman.

He jerked his thumb to the door on the left that led backstage.

I followed his directions and found myself in the maze of corridors that I'd been in only half an hour earlier. I set off in the direction of the dressing room thinking that he might be in there tidying up. As I got closer, I heard his voice inside. It sounded as if he was talking on the phone so, not wanting to interrupt his call, I waited in the corridor.

"You're outside?" he said. "You dozo, you should have bleeped me, I'd have let you in. I'll come out and get you . . . Yeah, me too, been looking forward to seeing you all day. Can't wait . . . No, it's been great. Really great, I wish you could have been here. But I'm ready for some time off. All I want to do now is spend the rest of the day with you. Maybe we could get a bite then go back to my place for a movie and chill out . . ." His voice got softer and deeper as the last sentence went on. There was no way he was talking to just a mate.

I felt a sinking feeling in the bottom of my

stomach and ran back down through the corridors, out into the studio and outside to find Lucy and Nesta.

"What's the matter?" asked Lucy when she saw my face.

I scanned the crowd that was still hanging about outside. I wondered which one she was. Gabriel's girlfriend.

"Gabriel. I just heard him arranging to meet his girlfriend," I groaned.

"How? When?" asked Nesta. "Are you sure?"

I nodded. "I heard him talking on the phone. And I could tell, not only by what he was saying but you know, by his tone of voice, it was all deep and smoochy . . ."

Lucy put her arm around me. "Oh, Izzie. I'm so sorry."

I bit my lip. I didn't want to blub in front of them. It had been such a brilliant day, the best ever and I'd really hoped that it was going to end with a date with Gabriel. Stupid, stupid, I told myself. Why do I have to go and fall for another boy who is already attached? And who had I been fooling thinking he'd feel the same way about me as I felt about him just because I'd sung a stupid song. How could he resist me? Easily.

"She's out here somewhere," I said, as I continued looking around. There were so many girls hanging about and then I spotted one apart from the crowd sitting on a wall. She looked as though she was waiting for someone as she didn't appear to be with anyone from the show. She was tall, blonde and had cut-glass cheekbones. "I bet it's her. No. Don't look. Behind you, Nesta. But don't stare."

Nesta did a casual look around, scanning the area. "Maybe," she said. "Could be her. She's classy-looking and we all know that Gabriel has taste."

Yeah, I thought. Whatever made me think that he'd pick a dud like me? So I can sing. So what?

A moment later, the stage door opened and Gabriel came out. He too scanned the crowd, then saw me and came straight over.

"Izzie," he said. "What a day, huh? You were *so* good. You must feel brilliant after that."

Lucy and Nesta were scowling at him and I hoped Nesta didn't butt in and say something awful. No one was to know that he was already attached and it wasn't as though we'd snogged or anything. It wasn't like it had been with Jay. Gabriel hadn't lied to me.

Gabriel put his arm round me and gave me a squeeze. "But listen, Izzie. Stay in touch, hey? I'd like to hear more of your songs. And you know where I live now so come over whenever you feel like it. I meant it about wanting my place to be an open house."

I thought I heard Nesta growl as I felt my heart sink even further. Maybe he was like Jay. Another cheater.

"But what about your girlfriend?"

"*Girl*friend! What girlfriend?" he asked.

"I heard you. I . . . I wasn't eavesdropping or anything, I . . . er, came looking for you to say goodbye and you were on the phone talking to your girlfriend."

Gabriel looked taken aback. "When?"

"Back in the dressing room. Just now."

Gabriel looked really puzzled then he laughed. "Oh, God. I'm so sorry . . . I assumed that you knew . . ."

"Knew what?"

"*Boy*friend," he said. "I'm gay. I was talking to my boyfriend."

Just at that moment, a stunning looking boy with short dark hair and chiselled features came over.

"Hey, Andy," said Gabriel. "Come and meet Iz and her mates."

I wanted to die.

# Chapter 16

# Dear
## Izzie . . .

"So the singles' club meets once again," I said. "Will I never learn?"

"You weren't to know," said TJ.

"*I* should have known," said Nesta. "The signs were all there. He was too good to be true."

It was the following Friday and we were hanging out at TJ's, helping her with the last minute changes to the magazine. She'd been working on an article called "Dieting Makes you Fat," and she wanted comments from me seeing as I'm now our resident diet expert.

"I think diets make you fat because the night before you go on one, you binge as you think you can never eat anything naughty-but-nice ever again. And then after a few days or a week of denial, you get bored or hungry so you break the diet. Then you feel bad, think oh I must get back on my diet, I'll start on Monday and this time be really, really strict . . . but on Sunday, I'll have my last treat ever and the cycle starts again. If people just ate normally but less, it would work much better than all that yo-yo-ing."

Nesta gave me the thumbs-up. "Sounds like you've seen sense my leettle curvy chum," she said.

I gave her the thumbs-up back. I felt that I'd found some balance in my life again and I didn't feel so bad about Gabriel anymore. I'd already been over to his place in the week and we'd had a good laugh about it all and what's more, I feel like I've found a new mate. And what more could you ask for, a friend who's a boy but who has immaculate taste in everything from makeup and dress sense to décor. As Nesta had said, the perfect boy.

"Anyway, we can't be the singles' club," said TJ, "because Lucy's not really single are you Luce?"

Lucy blushed. "Yes, I am."

"So why were you snogging Tony last time you were at our flat? I saw you," said Nesta.

Lucy squirmed in her seat. "Oh *then*? Um . . . er . . ."

"So are you getting back with him or not?" I asked.

"I've *told* you," she said. "No. But that doesn't mean we can't have the occasional snog or see a movie. He agrees. Just friends. He's got his A-levels coming up so he's going to have to work really hard. He said no way is he getting involved with anyone new as the last thing he needs are distractions or complications or new girlfriends going all emotional on him. With us, it's comfortable. We can hang out. We know what to expect from each other. We give each other space. I understand he has to study. He understands that I don't want to get into a heavy involvement so there it is. Sorted. We can enjoy the last few months before he goes off to whichever university in September."

I laughed. Some things never change. Lucy and Tony will probably be meeting up for the occasional snog or movie when they're old age pensioners.

"And hey, Iz, you needn't be single if you don't

want," said Nesta. "I saw Chris last night and apparently Tawny dumped Jay last weekend. She saw Liam's photos of Italy and there were some of you in there so she put two and two together. Chris said that he was asking after you."

"No thanks," I said. "Been there, done that. If he cheated on Tawny, how would I know he wasn't going to cheat on me? Some boys you just can't trust and I'm not going through that again."

"Good for you, Iz," said Lucy.

"What about you, Nesta?" I asked. "There were so many boys on the show ogling you. Anyone you want to ogle back?"

Nesta sighed. "Nah. I'm going through a particularly barren time with boys lately. I don't want one just for the sake of it. It's too boring. To tell you the truth, I've been enjoying being single. As Tony said, no complications. I'd rather hang out with you guys for the moment."

Lucy mocked fainting. "Are you ill, Nesta?"

Nesta punched her. "No, I'm not. I just don't want to waste my time and I don't want to compromise. No, next time I date a boy, it's going to be the real thing or nothing at all."

TJ, Lucy, and I all exchanged doubtful looks.

"I give her a week," said TJ.

"O ye of little faith," said Nesta. "There is more to life than boys, you know."

"Now I *know* she's ill," I said. "Don't worry love, we'll take care of you. You'll be as right as rain in no time."

"Hey how's the diet going, Iz?" asked Lucy.

"It's not a diet, it's a healthy eating plan," I replied. "Didn't you hear my comments for TJ's article? Dieting makes you fat."

"Ooo, get her," said Lucy, laughing.

"But actually I've lost three pounds already."

I'd been back to the club and weighed in and at first I was disappointed that I hadn't lost more but then Shirley had shown us this great lump of fat. It was enormous, like a huge blob of butter.

"That's just two pounds," she'd said.

It didn't seem so bad after that. Somehow though, my weight didn't feel like such a big issue anymore. Since *Teen Talk* last Saturday, loads of people had come up to me from school and even a few boys in the street who had seen the show. All of them had complimented me on my performance and no one had said I'd looked like a great fairy elephant.

I was feeling a lot better about things. I know that having the perfect body is not what it's all about and I know that no one's ever happy; if not with their legs, it's their tum or their hair or their bum. You can't let it ruin your life. Not that that is going to stop me going to my Weight Winners class. I want to continue because I want to get back into my old clothes, but now I feel that I'm doing it for me—to feel good, not to fit in with what I think some boy wants. And the plan does seem to work, even though it sometimes feels like I'm eating a lot. Already, my clothes feel looser and the outfit from Cyberdog looks fantastic. I'm looking forward to going out partying in it and not feeling like I have to hide myself away at home, my life on hold, waiting until I'm skinny. I've learned some valuable stuff about food—mainly that I don't have to starve myself to lose weight. Learning to eat the right foods is the way, whereas starvation is just a waste of time.

Just as I was getting ready to leave TJ's, my phone rang.

"Hi, Izzie, it's Gabriel. I'm at the studio. Can you come over?"

"Sure," I said. "I'm with the girls. Shall we all come?"

"Yeah, sure. I've got something to show you."

"What?"

"Aha, you'll see."

He wouldn't tell me any more than that, so we set off, wondering what he wanted.

When we arrived at the studio, we waited in the reception area while the girl behind the desk let him know that we were there. He came out a few minutes later. He was carrying a large envelope.

"So what's the big mystery?" I asked.

Gabriel grinned and beckoned us to sit on one of the sofas by a coffee table where he produced a wad of letters from the envelope. "Thought you might like to see some of these," he said.

I sat next to him on the sofa and TJ, Nesta, and Lucy crowded round to look.

"Ohmigod," said Nesta. "They're fan letters."

Gabriel grinned again. "They've been filtering in all week. Looks like you're a hit, Izzie Foster."

TJ, Lucy and Nesta all took a small pile each, sat down and we began to read.

"*Dear Iz*," read Lucy, "*I think you are the most beautiful girl in the world and what a voice . . .*"

"*Dear Ms. Foster,*" read Nesta, "*I wonder if you would do me the honour of accompanying me on a date. I enclose a picture . . .*" She had a quick look at the enclosed photo. "Eeew, I don't think so."

I took the photo from her. The man in it was old enough to be my father, no—my stepfather, as Angus is older than Dad.

"*Dear Izzie,*" read TJ. "*I love you, will you marry me?*"

It was amazing. Letter after letter. My first fan mail. I would treasure it forever.

"*Dear Iz,*" read Nesta. "Oh . . . no, you don't want to read this one. A bit rude, but I think the gist of it is that he fancies you."

Gabriel took the letter off her. "You always get the odd nutter in there but wow, Izzie. How do these make you feel?"

I beamed out at them all. "Pretty darned blooming amazing," I said.

"I think that means good," said Lucy. "And we don't ever, ever want to hear again that you think you are a great fat ugly lump."

"You won't," I said. "I promise."

And I meant it.

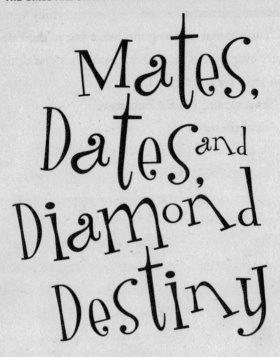

# Mates, Dates and Diamond Destiny

by Cathy Hopkins

"I bet he's only doing it to meet girls," I said as I buttoned up my jacket to keep out the chilly wind that had blown up whilst we were inside the café.

"Who? What?" asked Lucy.

"That William boy . . ."

"I knew you liked him," said Lucy.

"Pound," said Izzie.

"A pound? Whose side are you on?" I asked.

"You said boy," said Izzie.

"You're supposed to be my mate, not Tony's, so forget about that stupid bet, will you?"

"But we promised to be witnesses," said Izzie.

I wrapped my arm around her neck and pulled back slightly. "And I promise that I will kill you if you don't forget it. Understand, *amigo*?"

"Understand," spluttered Izzie. "So what were you saying?"

"William. I reckon he only does that collecting money for charity to pull girls."

"No," said Izzie. "I disagree. He's too good looking. He wouldn't need to pull a stunt like that to get a girl."

"Looks don't necessarily ensure you pull," I said. "You have to meet people too and it helps if you have a ready-made opener. He's on to a winner there, I reckon. Yes. Very clever indeed. I should put it on my list of pulling techniques after get yourself a dog."

"A dog?" asked Lucy.

"Yeah. Look at all the attention we get when we take Ben and Jerry out. Or Mojo."

Lucy laughed. "We get attention all right when they've put their noses somewhere they shouldn't be."

"Dogs are a ready-made introduction," I said, "whether they're well-behaved or not. It's the same with collecting for charity. It gives you an excuse to approach cute boys that you might otherwise be shy of."

"But you're not shy," said Lucy.

"I am sometimes," I said.

Lucy looked at Izzie as if to say she didn't believe it one bit.

TJ came out of the shop. "What have I missed?"

"Nesta saying that she thought William did his charity work as a way of meeting girls," said Izzie.

"No way," said TJ. "No one could be that calculating, could they?"

Izzie and Lucy looked accusingly at me.

"What?" I said. "*What?*"

"*You're* that calculating," said Izzie. "You're thinking of doing it as a way of meeting boys."

"And what's wrong with that, Miss High and Mighty?" I asked. "You can do good *and* meet people at the same time. And what's wrong with being calculating about meeting boys? Sometimes you have to have a plan. Life is what you make it. And if you do charity, people automatically think you're a good person, so that's a bonus as well."

TJ looked shocked and shook her head. "I'm not sure about that," she said. "It sounds cold. Like you're using people to make yourself look better."

"No way," I objected. "No way am I a user."

"Yeah. But don't you think your intentions are supposed to be more sincere?" asked Lucy.

I had a feeling that they were ganging up on me again. I was being cast in a bad light and all because I tried to think up good ways to meet boys. It was so unfair – actually, they should be grateful that I'm so creative in my boy-meeting technique!

"I *am* sincere," I said. "I just like meeting boys and this seems like a good way. Two birds with one stone sort of thing."

# truth or dare

By the bestselling author of the Mates, Dates series,

## Cathy Hopkins

Meet Cat, Becca, Squidge, Mac, and Lia. These girls and guys are totally tight—and totally obsessed with the game of truth or dare . . . even when it reveals too much!

Every book is a different dare . . . and a fun new adventure.

### Read them all:

## White Lies and Barefaced Truths

## The Princess of Pop

## Teen Queens and Has-Beens

## Starstruck

 ## Double Dare

From Simon Pulse
Published by Simon & Schuster

# ❀ WANTED ❀

## Single Teen Reader in search of a FUN romantic comedy read!

*How Not to Spend Your Senior Year*
BY CAMERON DOKEY

*Royally Jacked*
BY NIKI BURNHAM

*Ripped at the Seams*
BY NANCY KRULIK

*Cupidity*
BY CAROLINE GOODE

*Spin Control*
BY NIKI BURNHAM

*South Beach Sizzle*
BY SUZANNE WEYN & DIANA GONZALEZ

*She's Got the Beat*
BY NANCY KRULIK

*30 Guys in 30 Days*
BY MICOL OSTOW

Available from Simon Pulse ★ Published by Simon & Schuster

♥ ❀ ♥ ❀ ♥ ❀ ♥ ❀ ♥ ❀ ♥ ❀ ♥ ❀

**BY THE BESTSELLING AUTHOR OF THE MATES, DATES SERIES CATHY HOPKINS**

# Mates, Dates Guide

## To Life, Love, and Looking Luscious

WHAT HAPPENS WHEN LUCY, NESTA, IZZIE, AND T. J. GET TOGETHER AND START TALKING?

THEY COME UP WITH ALL SORTS OF SOLUTIONS FOR LIFE'S LITTLE DILEMMAS. . . .

Like boys for a start: what they want, where to find them, how to be a great kisser—everything you really need to know. They also share loads of lifestyle tips, from achieving the essential wardrobe to how to deal with a bad hair day.

From Simon Pulse
Published by
Simon & Schuster

**The Mates, Dates girls are dishing all their secrets . . . just for you!**

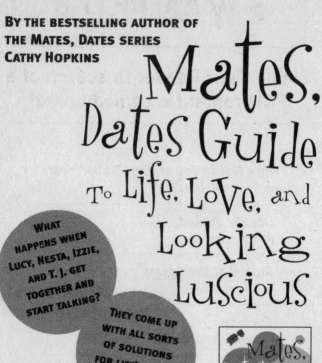